Five years.
Suddenly it seemed like forever.

It had been so long since he had seen her, and yet he would have recognized that graceful walk anywhere. The smile given so freely to strangers. It suddenly struck him how much he missed that smile. It had been hard to come by as their marriage had crumbled.

And now here she was not ten feet away.

"Any updates?" she asked as she moved Isabella's backpack to the floor and started to sit. She glanced at him for the first time and was clearly prepared to nod pleasantly when her eyes went wide and her body froze.

Tom gave her an uncertain smile as he basked in the sheer pleasure of being near enough to touch her after all this time.

"Surprise," he said quietly as he closed the cover of his computer.

Books by Anna Schmidt

Steeple Hill Love Inspired

Caroline and the Preacher
A Mother for Amanda
The Doctor's Miracle
Love Next Door
Matchmaker, Matchmaker...
Lasso Her Heart
Mistletoe Reunion

Love Inspired Historical

Seaside Cinderella

ANNA SCHMIDT

Anna Schmidt is a two-time finalist for the coveted RITA® Award from the Romance Writers of America, as well as twice a finalist for the *Romantic Times BOOKreviews* Reviewer's Choice Award. The most recent was for her 2006 novel, *Matchmaker, Matchmaker....* The sequel, *Lasso Her Heart,* has inspired readers to write to Anna via her Web site (www.booksbyanna.com) and declare that its theme of recovery from tragedy brought them comfort in their own lives. Her novel *The Doctor's Miracle* was the 2002 *Romantic Times BOOKreviews* Reviewer's Choice Inspirational category winner. A transplant from Virginia, she now calls Wisconsin home—escaping the tough winters in Florida.

Mistletoe Reunion
Anna Schmidt

Steeple
Hill®

Published by Steeple Hill Books™

STEEPLE HILL BOOKS

Steeple
Hill®

Recycling programs
for this product may
not exist in your area.

ISBN-13: 978-0-373-81387-2
ISBN-10:   0-373-81387-2

MISTLETOE REUNION

www.SteepleHill.com

Printed in U.S.A.

Except the Lord build the house, they labor
in vain that build it: except the Lord keep the city,
the watchman waketh but in vain.

—*Psalms* 127:1

To everyone who knows the true power that growing up in a small town can have no matter how large the place you end up calling home.

Chapter One

"It's snowing!" Isabella crowed as the flight from Phoenix landed in Denver. "Look at the roof of the terminal. It's like snow-capped mountains. How totally cool!"

Norah Wallace could not help smiling. Was it just a mere forty-eight hours earlier that her thirteen-year-old daughter was fighting the very idea of a trip to Wisconsin to visit her grandparents for Thanksgiving? Obviously she'd changed her mind, but Norah was quickly learning not to spend too much time questioning the logic of teenagers.

While Isabella reveled in the sight of the unique fabric tension roof of the terminal, Norah noticed snow falling in huge flakes that covered everything—including the runway—in a duvet of white. "Hopefully it won't delay our connection to Chicago," Norah said.

"Oh, Mom, you worry about the weirdest things. What could be so bad about getting stuck in Colorado? We could go skiing."

"No one is going skiing—at least not in Colorado," Norah said. "And I don't worry about everything. I just want things to go smoothly." She felt the familiar twinge of guilt that came with her impatience and covered it by rummaging through her carry-on. Did her daughter think she wanted to be the one always throwing cold water on Izzy's flights of fancy? No. But she was raising Izzy on her own—well, not on her own. Her father—Norah's ex—was still very involved. But Izzy lived with her in Arizona, not with Tom in California.

She checked their schedule. "We have an hour layover here and it looks like our connecting flight is in the same concourse, so we should have time for something to eat." It was an attempt at conciliation, but Izzy was slumped down in the seat, staring out the window.

"Whatever," she muttered.

The minute the flight attendant announced permission to use cell phones, Isabella went to work. Norah marveled at the way her daughter's thumbs danced on the keypad as the plane taxied to a gate. Everyone scrambled to gather belongings as if life itself depended on their quick exit from the plane. She stood in the aisle and watched Izzy transcribe messages to all her friends. Norah could barely manage e-mail. How did these kids learn these technically complicated things so quickly?

When their turn came to exit, Izzy dropped her phone in her pocket and hefted her backpack over one shoulder as they entered the concourse and joined throngs of other travelers making their way to and from restrooms, shops and gates. Norah couldn't help noticing that Izzy seemed to be looking for something and took some comfort in the fact that her daughter's annoyance was short-lived. But then as usual Izzy threw her a curveball she wasn't prepared for.

"Are you ever sorry you divorced Dad?" Isabella asked as they wove their way through crowds of passengers and dodged electric carts.

"First of all, the decision was mutual," Norah replied, fighting her natural instinct to remind Izzy an airport was neither the time nor place for this discussion.

"And second of all?" Isabella asked.

"Oh honey, you know the story. We each wanted different things." *Quell the impatience,* she reminded herself. She draped her free arm over Izzy's bony shoulders. "Well, actually we wanted the same thing—to make sure you had the best possible life."

"So how come the two of you couldn't figure it out together?"

"Timing—meant to be." Norah tossed off clichés as she searched for an answer that would end the conversation. The older Isabella got, the harder that challenge became.

"Yeah, so Dad took off for San Francisco like opening a branch law office there was a good idea or something," Isabella said wearily, "and you stayed in the desert because working on the reservation was somehow so important." She frowned. "So will one of you please explain how doing what you wanted was best for me?"

"Trust me. It was. We've remained friends— your father and I—not like some couples."

"Friends see each other now and then. When's the last time you actually saw Daddy? Not talked on the phone, but were face-to-face?"

"It just hasn't—that is—" Norah stumbled for words. *Five years ago.* She considered whether or not to tell Izzy that she remembered the exact moment she'd last seen Tom. He'd been walking away from her to get in a cab and head for California.

"Ooh—soft pretzels." And Izzy was off. Obviously the moment had passed.

"For lunch?" Norah shifted her bag and hurried after her daughter.

"Mother! We're on holiday. Live a little," Isabella said hooking her arm through Norah's and steering her toward the pretzel stand.

As soon as his plane touched down in Denver, Tom called Isabella's cell phone. He wanted to be sure she'd let Norah know he was going to Normal for the holiday. Voice mail. Knowing his daughter, she had forgotten so just to be sure Norah got the message, Tom decided to call the house in Arizona.

He waited for the beep of the old-fashioned answering machine Norah still used even though Isabella had tried to persuade her that voice mail was ever so much more efficient. "But we have the machine and it's paid for," Norah had explained according to Izzy, "so why would I incur a monthly expense to switch to voice mail?"

Tom smiled as he recalled Bella's growl of frustration at her mother's well-known practicality and maddening logic. For his part he had always admired Norah's determination not to jump on the technology bandwagon, although he couldn't help believing that as time went by and technology continued to advance, it was at least partly her stubbornness that had made her avoid such conveniences. Norah could be very stubborn.

"Norah?" he said when he realized the beep had sounded. "Tom here." *Like she wouldn't recognize your voice?* "In case Bella forgot to pass the message, just letting you know—well, Clare called and you know my sister. She had this brainstorm for us to celebrate Mom and Dad's fiftieth this weekend instead of for their actual anniversary in January, so I'll be in Wisconsin if you need to reach me. I'll be back late Sunday night. Bella was a little vague on your plans for the holiday, but I hope it's a good one." As always when he left messages for her, he paused. It seemed as if he wanted to say something more, but in five years he had not been able to figure out what. "Bye," he added quickly and hung up.

He picked up messages his assistant had left him as he walked to his connecting gate, then called back to answer her questions. The plane from California had spent several precious minutes circling the airport and now he just hoped he wouldn't miss the flight to Chicago.

As he hung up, the gate was in sight and packed with people waiting. He scanned the rows of chairs for a place to drop his luggage and spotted an empty one right next to a girl waving wildly at him.

Bella? Here? In Denver?

"Dad!" Isabella stood on the chair. "Dad! Over here."

Tom eased his way through the disorganized parade of people, his smile meeting Isabella's while his eyes searched for Norah.

"Dad," Isabella cried for the third time as she catapulted her way into his arms. "Surprise! How cool is this?"

Tom laughed and eased his daughter back to a standing position. "What are you doing here?" He glanced around again. "Where's your mother?"

"Bathroom. She is going to seriously freak," Isabella predicted.

"Where are you two headed?" Tom was pretty sure he knew. Norah rarely took time off and when she did, it was to go to Wisconsin to see her parents.

"To see the grands." The response was muffled and Isabella was looking somewhere over his left shoulder.

"Bella, you didn't tell your mom that I was also going to Normal?"

Isabella had the good sense to look slightly abashed. "I kind of forgot."

Tom raised his eyebrows.

"Look at it this way—now we can all celebrate Thanksgiving and the anniversary together. How cool is that?"

"What do you think your mom will have to say about this?"

Isabella's expression tightened and she sighed dramatically. "Did it ever occur to you guys that the longer you keep up this thing of never seeing each other like up close and personal, the harder it's going to be when it actually happens?"

Tom considered the best response to that, but Isabella was on a roll.

"I mean the very fact that neither one of you has found someone new should prove something," she added. "Like maybe splitting up was a mistake of astronomical proportions?"

"I thought you said your mom was dating."

"Well, she didn't join a convent after you two split, Dad." Isabella rolled her eyes at him. "And you haven't exactly been without your share of female companionship. What was the last one's name? Tabitha?" she added.

"Tamara," he corrected, "and she was—is a business associate."

"Whatever. She's a lot younger than you. What was that about?"

"We work together on various projects. Her age has nothing to do with it."

Isabella's smirk said she was not convinced. "You want to know what I think?"

"Why do I feel you're going to tell me whether I want to know or not?"

"I think that you and mom both miss each other, but you're both too stubborn to admit it and try again. That's why you've spent the last five years finding ways not to see each other."

"Bella, it's been a long time," Tom explained, hating the fact that he was throwing cold water on her hope for a reconciliation. "We're different people now."

"Ya think?" she said with a dramatic sigh as if grown-ups were just dumber than dirt. "Okay. I didn't forget," she admitted, casting her eyes heavenward. "Forgive me," she whispered, then turned her attention back to her father.

On the occasion of her twelfth birthday Isabella had joined the church and her passion for her faith had blossomed from there. She sang in the youth choir, provided child care for toddlers for church events and was very active in the social action committee of her youth group.

"I'm surprised at you, Isabella," Tom said now. "I thought it was important to you to abide by the rules of your faith."

"Our faith, Dad. You used to belong to the same church and Mom still does."

"You know what I'm saying. How could you lie to your mother?"

"I didn't," she protested. "Not really."

"A lie of omission is still a lie," Tom reminded her.

Bella sighed and slumped back in her chair. "But where's the harm? I mean, how cool is it going to be to surprise Mom with the fact that we're all going to Normal together? Even I never imagined we'd actually be able to hook up here— though I have to admit I hoped we might."

"As I recall, your mom is not overly fond of surprises," Tom reminded her as he set his carry-on and computer bag on the small table next to her chair and tried to figure out the next steps in the farce his only child had created.

Isabella blinked. "Yeah, well... Too late now— she'll be back any minute." She eyed Tom warily. "Are you going to like disappear?"

"No, I'm here. You're here. Let's see how it goes."

Isabella grinned and stood up to clear a chair for him. "Okay, so come over here and sit down," she instructed. "Have you got something to read? No, better yet, open your computer—that's good." Isabella danced around him choreographing the surprise for Norah. "Here she comes," she whispered and giggled as she buried her face in a fashion magazine.

Norah was still several yards away, but he instantly picked her out of the masses and time reversed as he recalled the moment he'd realized he was in love with her. She had been a high school junior and he was a senior. She had lived just down the block from him her entire life. They had waited together at the same bus stop, attended the same church, seen each other countless times in all seasons because their parents were the best of friends. And yet, had he ever really looked at her until that winter's day when he stood shivering next to his broken-down car waiting for his dad to come and rescue him?

She'd been with a gang of her girlfriends, laughing and gabbing the way teenaged girls did, when one of them had spotted him. That girl had nudged Norah and nodded in his direction. Norah had peeled away from the others and headed his way.

"Problem?" The way she said it he thought she was getting a kick out his misery.

"Not if you've got a set of jumper cables in your backpack," he fired back.

Her eyes had widened in surprise. "You don't have jumper cables?"

Tom had seen no reason to respond to the obvious. Instead of moving on, she had leaned against the car with him. "Want me to call my dad?"

"No."

"Well, no need to be rude," she'd muttered, then, "Oh, you called your dad."

His father had pulled up then and produced the necessary cables to jump-start Tom's car. "You okay from here?" he asked when the car fired and continued to idle. "I have to get back to work."

"Yeah. Thanks, Pop."

Norah had still been standing there after his dad drove away. "You need a ride or something?"

"Are you going home?"

Tom had sighed. "No, I thought as long as I got the thing running I'd take a drive to California. Yes, I'm going home. Get in."

She had and then just after he'd pulled into traffic, she started laughing. This girl was laughing at Tom Wallace—student council president, varsity quarterback, on his way to university. "What?" he'd barked.

"Your ears are like Rudolph's nose," she'd managed. "I mean they are seriously red. They have these things now called hats, you know."

He'd glanced at himself in the rearview mirror. She had a point. He found himself grinning and then they were both laughing.

"Here," she said and pulled off her own knit stocking cap and pulled it over his hair and ears. Her warmth was still there in the yarn.

He'd dropped her off at her house, handed her back her hat and asked if she had a date for the winter dance. And she had answered by asking a question of her own. "Are you asking me to go with you?"

"Yeah."

"Then ask," she'd said.

That was Norah—straightforward, self-confident, and sometimes too sure that she was in the right. *Like when she refused to even consider the move to San Francisco.*

"She's coming," Bella hissed. "Look busy."

Over the open cover of his computer, Tom watched Norah approach. *Five years.* Suddenly it seemed like forever. What would he say to her after so much time? It wasn't as if they hadn't spoken. The one thing they had both agreed upon was that Izzy's welfare and happiness came before any conflict or battle scars they might have with each other. But what to say face-to-face?

It had been so long since he had seen her and yet he would have recognized that graceful walk anywhere. The smile given so freely to total strangers. It suddenly struck him how much he had missed that smile. It had been hard to come by as their marriage had crumbled. Not that he had been giving her his best either. He'd been angry and hurt and looking hard for somewhere to lay the blame and guilt he felt creeping over him. He felt a little of it now, but maturity made him recognize it for what it was. Trying to make the fact they hadn't seen each other for five long years her fault.

And now here she was not ten feet away, stopping to retrieve a child's toy and return it with a goofy face that made the kid laugh. He had less than a minute to figure out some snappy line. His hands were shaking slightly. She looked great. She was one of those fortunate women who would age beautifully. He saw a couple of male passengers in the waiting area glance her way and felt a prick of the jealousy mixed with pride he'd always felt whenever they went somewhere together.

"Any updates?" she asked as she moved Isabella's backpack to the floor and started to sit. He could smell the familiar perfume of her hair, her skin. He could see the little scar that ran just in front of her left ear. She glanced at him and was prepared to nod pleasantly when her eyes went wide and her body froze.

Tom gave her an uncertain smile as he basked in the sheer pleasure of being near enough to touch her after all this time. Same dark hair—different style. Sort of a tousled cap of curls. Skin—unblemished except for the two spots of high color that currently dotted her cheeks. Eyes? Ah, those eyes. The blue-green color of a clear water lake—deep enough to swim in, get lost in.

"Surprise," he said quietly as he closed the cover of his computer.

Chapter Two

Norah could not have been more surprised if the president himself had been sitting next to her. Her lips twitched, but her voice seemed frozen as a number of catchy comebacks rocketed through her brain.

Gee, obviously the last five years have been great to you—you look...

Well, imagine this—

Tom Wallace, how long has it been? Let's see, must be five years, three months and twelve days or something like that.

Izzy bounced to her knees on the chair to Norah's left and rescued her. "Do you believe this? I mean what are the odds that we'd all end up in the same airport at the same time and waiting on the same plane?"

"Pretty good given the fact you knew I was

coming this way, young lady," Tom said, but his eyes never left Norah's face.

Her gaze shifted to Isabella. "You knew?"

"Sorta, kinda," Izzy said and looked down.

Norah blinked, her thick black lashes feathering her cheeks. "Isabella Wallace, I am surprised at you." She realized she could not avoid acknowledging Tom's presence forever, so she took a deep breath and plastered on her biggest smile. "How are you, Tom?" she asked as if they were former classmates who had run into each other unexpectedly.

"Good. Fine," he said, clearing his throat. "You?"

"Fine," she said.

Isabella made a face and they both heard her sigh of frustration. The sigh brought Norah's attention back to her daughter. "You should go to the restroom," she said.

"Mom," Izzy moaned. "Stop treating me like I'm eight. I know when I do and don't have to go, okay?"

Isabella had been just about to celebrate her eighth birthday when the divorce papers arrived. Norah had had the phone in hand ready to call and put Izzy on the line so she could tell her father all about the party that Norah had arranged. In those early weeks and months she had remained in shock. It seemed impossible that she and Tom— of all people—had gone their separate ways.

The airport public address system crackled to life. "They're calling first class," Norah translated the garbled message and nodded toward the open door leading to the jetway.

He smiled. "I'm in coach. Busiest travel day of the year—you know how it goes."

"You can sit with us," Isabella said.

Simultaneously Norah and Tom opened their mouths to object to that idea.

"The plane is packed, honey," Norah said.

"We're running late, Bella. Let's not complicate things," Tom said.

Norah glanced his way, acknowledging with a slight nod of her head that he had backed her up. But then they had always been a team when it came to their daughter. The one thing they had both held sacred was that whatever differences they had, those would not affect Isabella any more than they had already.

She's still so young and lots of her classmates have divorced parents, they had both rationalized. In time, surely....

"Why did you decide to travel under such circumstances?" she asked. "No one's ill, are they?" she asked alarmed and saw that familiar flicker of irritation because he took her comment wrong. No doubt he thought that she was implying that the only thing that could drag Tom away from his work on a moment's notice had to be something to do with his parents. Most of their arguments in those last months together had been about his devotion, or as she saw it obsession, with his career.

"Clare and Liz got this idea that we should all surprise Mom and Dad over Thanksgiving for their fiftieth," he replied. "You know Clare. Once she gets an idea it's easier to let her have her way than try to debate the timing of the idea."

"Aunt Liz is coming, too? And the cousins?" Isabella clapped her hands in delight. "I mean is this the best Thanksgiving or what?"

The gate agent called Norah and Isabella's row. Norah busied herself gathering her things and organizing Izzy's belongings in her backpack.

"We could share a car when we get to Chicago," Tom said.

"I've already reserved one," she replied and then immediately added. "Of course, I could cancel it. Yes, sharing a car would be nice. Thanks."

"Okay, so see you in Chicago," he said as he hugged Izzy.

"You and your father can talk more there," Norah promised Izzy as she hurried her toward the gate.

You and your father...meaning what? She didn't intend to say anything?

She glanced back wanting to apologize for what he might have thought she was implying, but Tom was packing his computer, his back to her.

"I have to go to the bathroom," Isabella announced as soon as they had located their seats and she had stowed her backpack under the seat nearest the window leaving Norah with the middle.

"I warned you," Norah said, but stood aside, blocking boarding passengers so Isabella could make her way to the rear of the plane. She sat down again and bent to rearrange their belongings so that she would have some legroom. When she looked up Tom was standing in the aisle waiting for other passengers ahead of him to get settled.

"I'm in the back," he said, making a face.

Norah shook her head sympathetically. "I'm in the middle," she replied, indicating the obvious. It was the kind of banter they'd always been good at and a little of the initial tension between them eased. During their marriage they'd had a long-running debate about which was worse—back of the plane with its noise and turbulence or crushed between two passengers who seemed to think they had claim to all armrests.

"Trade you?"

Norah smiled. "Not a chance."

Tom moved on just as the crew chief announced another slight delay to allow passengers on a late-arriving plane to make their connection.

A large man carrying a briefcase, carry-on luggage and an overcoat opened and slammed several filled overhead compartments. Norah pulled the airline magazine from the seatback pocket and flipped through it hoping he had the vacant seat across the aisle.

No such luck. He forced the luggage into an overhead bin two rows ahead of them, then threw his coat onto the seat and sat down heavily, his bulk and the coat spilling over into Norah's space as he jammed the briefcase under the seat in front of him.

Norah nodded at him as she gently pushed his coat off the armrest they shared. The man ignored her.

"Hey, Mom," Isabella said. "Guess what?" Izzy was accompanied by a young woman with a toddler in tow and what looked like a newborn cradled in her arms.

"This is Emma and she's got the two seats next to Dad and she'd be willing to switch, so I said that would be great—I'll even take the middle."

Norah tried not to take perverse pleasure in the look of pleading horror the businessman gave her. "You'll take the middle?"

"Yeah, come on."

"Excuse me," Norah said sweetly as she recovered her purse and Isabella's backpack and stood.

"But," the man protested as Norah slid past him.

"Everything all right here?" the male flight attendant asked.

"Perfect," Isabella exclaimed. "My dad's back there and this nice lady traded so that now we get to sit together and—"

"Okay, I just need everyone to get settled as soon as possible. We're about to close the cabin door."

Tom was standing in the aisle waiting for them. Norah tried not to stare at the way his hair— brown streaked with copper—was still thick and silky. She did not meet his chocolate-brown eyes, fixed on her as she slid next to the window and Isabella took the middle without protest.

"You put her up to that—switching," Norah said.

"What?" Tom's eyes were wide with innocence.

"It was my idea, Mom," Isabella said. "Honestly."

Norah had her doubts.

"How are your folks?" Tom asked politely once they were buckled in.

"Fine," Norah answered equally as polite. This

was going to be interminable. Suddenly she was glad to be in the back where the engine noise would surely make conversation impossible.

"This is going to be so great," Isabella exclaimed, ignoring the tension between her parents. "I mean, just wait until we all show up together. They are going to seriously freak."

"How's work?" Tom asked Norah.

"Fine," she said and looked out the window as the plane slowly taxied toward the runway. She wondered if she could be capable of more than that one-word response to anything Tom might ask.

"Ladies and gentlemen, we apologize for the short delay, but we should be airborne in about twenty minutes."

There was a ripple of muttered comments. "It's sleeting," Norah said.

Tom leaned across Isabella's lap to look out. Norah could not help but be aware of the scent of his aftershave—familiar and at the same time exotic. "From the looks of that sky we just need to get going," he said as the plane inched forward in line. "You okay?" He glanced up at Norah and she knew that he was remembering how nervous she got when flying. She couldn't help being touched that he had remembered.

"Fine," she replied and then grimaced. "I seem to have the same answer for everything, don't I?"

"Well, yeah," Isabella said before Tom could answer. "You're acting like you're on a first date or something, Mom."

Tom leaned back in his seat. "And just what would you know about first dates, young lady?"

Isabella blushed and giggled. "Oh, Dad."

Norah reached for her purse and pulled out a Sudoku puzzle book.

"Mom!" Isabella protested, casting a sidelong look from the book to Tom.

"Are you any good at those puzzles?" Tom asked, ignoring Isabella.

Norah shrugged. "Not really, but I can usually manage the simple ones."

"Can I try?" Tom asked, holding out his hand for the book.

Norah passed him the soft-covered book and held out her pencil.

Tom pulled a pen from his pocket and grinned. "No guts, no glory," he said and settled in to work the puzzle with Isabella's help.

Norah watched as he clicked the pen on and off—his hand tan against the pale cream starched cuff of his shirt. He wore dark brown casual slacks and a pullover sweater in a sort of copper shade that accented his tan and highlighted the gold flecks in his eyes. She heard his deep voice consulting with Isabella on an entry, his laughter when Isabella stopped him from making a mistake. He bent forward and ran his free hand through his hair. When a lock fell over his forehead, she literally had to tighten her grip on the armrest to resist the urge to smooth it back into place as she would have before.

Before. When they were married. When they were—

"Mom!"

Norah blinked. "Sorry," she said softly, still caught up in the fantasy of who she and Tom had once been to each other.

"I said, can you see what's happening? Why aren't we moving?"

Norah turned her attention to the window. It was coated with sleet. "I can't see," she said and just then the plane made a slow turn to the right. "I think we might be—"

"Ladies and gentlemen, weather conditions have changed. We need to de-ice the wings before we can take off. Please feel free to move about the cabin for the time being. We'll be on our way as soon as possible."

This time a chorus of groans rolled through the cabin as passengers crowded the aisle, rearranging the contents of overhead bins, stretching as they commiserated about the inconveniences of modern travel. Tom took advantage of the extra space afforded by being in the last row across from the galley. "Come on, Bella, stretch your legs."

Isabella followed her father's lead in a series of calf stretches and knee bends. The crew toured the cabin offering packages of pretzels and promising full beverage service once they were airborne.

"Your turn," Tom said and held out his hand to Norah. Norah slid across the row and stood in the aisle without taking his hand. "Feels good," she said as she stretched her arms high over her head, her fingertips grazing the ceiling.

Isabella lifted the armrests on their row and stretched out across all three seats, her MP3 player earphones in place. She closed her eyes and bounced her head and shoulders to the music they couldn't hear.

"I'm going for a little walk," Norah said, suddenly uncomfortable to find herself standing next to Tom—far too near to Tom for comfort.

He grinned. "Just stay inside the plane," he called as she edged forward.

The truth was she needed some time to think about the impact of spending Thanksgiving three blocks away from Tom and his family. In fact, there was no doubt that they would be thrown together often once they were back in Normal.

His parents and hers belonged to the same church and were still close friends. Isabella would move easily between the two houses. Izzy's aunts and cousins would surely want to include Isabella in whatever extravaganza they were concocting for the anniversary. They would certainly include Norah's parents—and Norah—in the invitation as well.

The aisle was crowded with other passengers and the plane was not nearly long enough for Norah to stay away indefinitely. She glanced back and saw Tom talking to another passenger. Ahead stood the businessman glaring at her as the young mother tried in vain to soothe the newborn and the toddler, both of whom were crying now. The scene gave new meaning to "between a rock and a hard place" but by far the lesser of the two evils was to return to her seat.

Isabella had dozed off, so Norah perched on the aisle armrest. Tom finished his exchange with the passenger waiting to use the restroom and turned. He was standing toe to toe with her, his forearm resting against the overhead bin. He'd removed his sweater and rolled back the sleeves of his shirt.

"How was your walk?" he asked.

"Fine," she replied and then blushed. "Uneventful," she added with a slight smile.

Tom did not return her smile. Instead he studied her closely. "You look great, Norah," he said.

Norah ran a self-conscious hand through her hair. "I've been up since four and my—"

"Why do you do that?" he asked. "You never used to do that."

Norah fought a twinge of irritation. *I never used to doubt that a marriage I thought was forever could fall apart in a matter of months.* What did he know about her these days? "Do what?" she asked.

"Put yourself down. Someone pays you a compliment and you—"

"You know, Tom, it has been a number of years. I might have changed in that time."

"I expect we both have, but—"

"Izzy tells me you're seeing someone new," she interrupted, determined to turn the focus from herself to him.

"Izzy doesn't approve of my choice in female companionship," he said with a glance at their sleeping daughter.

Norah shrugged. "She just needs time."

"Speaking of time," Tom said clearing his throat. "Five years and not once seeing each other, Norah—it's a long time. How did that happen?" He leaned in to allow another passenger to pass. His face was closer to hers now. His eyes locked on hers and she saw that he looked tired.

"It's not like we weren't in touch," she countered. "I mean we were always on the phone or leaving messages about Izzy. I think we've done well by her, don't you?"

"Stop changing the subject. You didn't want to see me. Why?"

Norah shifted uncomfortably. "That was just at first. I mean it was all so fresh and we were both so vulnerable and I thought that maybe—"

"But to let not one, but five years pass?"

"It just happened, Tom. I didn't plan it and you could have just as easily—" She was whispering, keenly aware of others around them but equally aware that she could have been shouting and few other passengers would have cared. They were all that wrapped up in their own problems.

"Ladies and gentlemen, please return to your seats and fasten your seat belts."

This time the general chorus of commentary was filled with relief and even laughter as passengers returned to their seats and buckled up.

Norah tapped Isabella's leg. "Turn that off and fasten your seat belt," she instructed.

Isabella swung her legs around and did as she was told, only she took the obvious seat—the one by the window.

"I'll take the middle," Tom offered.

"No, I've got it," Norah said as she sat down,

lowered both armrests and fastened her seat belt. She picked up the puzzlebook Tom had left on his seat, waited for him to sit down and then handed it to him.

"Thanks." He took out his pen and concentrated on the puzzle as Isabella stared out the window.

After several moments she reported their progress. "I think we're going back to the terminal."

"That's impossible," Norah said, leaning across her to look out the window. But her daughter was right. "Now what?" Norah muttered.

"Ladies and gentlemen, we are returning to the gate area. We regret that the airport is being closed for the time being. A major winter storm is passing through the area and we had hoped to get away in front of it, but it's coming too fast. Once we are at the gate you may deplane and there will be airline personnel inside the terminal with more information. Please feel free to make use of your cell phones to notify those who may be meeting you in Chicago of this unexpected situation—and thank you once again for choosing—"

Chapter Three

Even before the announcement ended, Tom had his cell phone out dialing his office. When he got voice mail, he glanced at his watch and realized that everyone had already left for the holiday.

"I was hoping to get my assistant to work on finding us an alternate flight," he explained, noting Norah's raised eyebrows.

"I didn't ask," she said.

But you questioned, he thought. *You always used to think I was putting work ahead of you and Bella.* He covered his irritation by pulling his sweater back on as they waited their turn to leave the plane.

If the country's fifth busiest airport had seemed crowded before, it was in total chaos when they emerged from the jetway. Harried airport personnel tried in vain to reassure passengers. Most passengers were accepting their fate, while a few like the businessman who'd shared a row with the screaming babies were demanding to speak with higher authorities. "You have to do something," he shouted, his mouth inches from the face of the gate agent. "From the looks of things we could be here for hours."

"Sir," the gate agent explained, "look at that weather." She pointed to the large windows where visibility was near zero. "Unfortunately none of us is going anywhere until this storm passes and we can get the runways cleared."

"And how long will that take?" the man demanded.

"I don't know, sir. Only God knows the answer to that one."

"She's right," Isabella said as she and her parents edged past the angry man. "This is God's work. He's got something in mind here and I think I know what it is." She looked up at her parents, then linked arms with them to either side of her. "Now let's get some food. I am so starving."

"You and your mother take care of getting us something to eat," Tom said handing Isabella money. "I'm going to see about getting us a hotel room—rooms—" he clarified when Norah's head shot up and her wide eyes met his. "There is no way we're going to get out of here tonight."

"We'll meet back here then?" Norah asked and realized she was glad that Tom was there. Tom had always been able to make things happen without berating people to get what he wanted.

"Give me half an hour," he said and strode away.

"What should I get for Dad?" Izzy asked when they were finally close to ordering.

"Turkey wrap with brown mustard, no mayo, tomato, lettuce, no sprouts," Norah said as she gathered bottled drinks from the cooler. "Pasta salad if they have it. No chips unless they're baked." She glanced up to find Izzy grinning at her, her eyes wide with surprise. "What?"

"How do you know that? I mean the details?"

Norah shrugged. "Lucky guess," she murmured.

"Right," Isabella said softly and smiled as she repeated the order verbatim and multiplied it by three.

The cashier rang up the sale and Isabella peeled off two twenties from the bills Tom had given her, then waited for change.

Tom was waiting for them at the assigned spot. "Well, here's the deal," he reported. "The airport is bringing in buses to take people to hotels. I was able to book us one room—two queen beds," he assured Norah.

"But what about the party in Normal? The grands?" Isabella protested.

"Honey, be thankful your father was able to get us a room." *One room—with two beds, but still one room.*

"We do have another option—staying here," Tom said as if he'd read her mind. "It might be something we want to consider."

"All night?" Isabella exclaimed. "Now let's see—on the one hand we have a reserved hotel room with TV, room service and our own bathroom and on the other we could bunk down here. Gee, tough one, Dad."

"Staying here means we are here when they get a runway cleared. The hotel room I got is at least twenty-five miles away and in this weather getting here from there—"

"—could take hours," Norah finished his thought, then focused her attention on Isabella when she caught the look in Tom's eyes. When they'd been together they had laughed about the way they used to finish each other's sentences on a regular basis. *Is the next step that we start to look alike?* Tom had teased. Norah focused on Izzy. "Staying here gives us the best possible chance for getting to the grands," she explained.

Izzy rolled her eyes. "Whatever."

"Bella, attitude," Tom warned. "Hey, it'll be an adventure—like camping."

Isabella gave him the wide-eyed grin of a six-year-old. "Oh goody, can we build a campfire and tell ghost stories and make s'mores?"

Tom laughed and wrapped his arm around her. "Come on. Let's see if we can snag a couple of those cots." He nodded to the area where people had lined up as skycaps wheeled in carts with folding cots loaded on top.

"Maybe Izzy should wait here with me," Norah said, eyeing the desperation of the stranded mob.

"You don't think I'm going into that, do you?" Tom said, his eyebrows raised in mock surprise.

"Well, how else—"

"Come on, Bella."

Norah watched as Tom steered Izzy to a corner on the outskirts of the crowd. She saw him approach a man and his wife—each with a cot in tow. A conversation ensued and next thing Norah knew Tom and Izzy were coming her way each hauling a cot.

"But, how—" Norah stuttered.

"We made a trade," Izzy told her. "Dad gave them the hotel room. They handed over the cots. No problem." She looked adoringly at Tom as if the man had suddenly sprouted a cape and tights.

As Norah followed them down the concourse, she saw Tom nod pleasantly to gate agents and other passengers as if spending the night at the Denver airport was no big deal. At the airline's private lounge he punched in a code and opened the door, holding it for Izzy to wrangle her cot inside and then waiting for Norah. "Over here," he added, spotting a pair of chairs in the corner.

"Do you think they'll unload the luggage?" Norah asked as Tom and Izzy set up the cots and she distributed the lunch.

"Not likely," Tom replied, following her glance toward an older woman at the desk who was explaining that her husband's medications were packed in their checked luggage.

Norah watched the woman leave the desk as she bit into her sandwich.

"Hey," Tom said softly, "leave the social working to the airport staff, okay?"

You can't save the world, Norah, he had once shouted at her when they were arguing. But he wasn't shouting now. His tone was gentle and sympathetic and his eyes told her that he understood that she really wanted to help.

"This looks great," Tom said, turning his attention to the sandwich. "And you remembered the mustard," he said.

"Mom remembered," Isabella replied before Norah could.

"Did you remember your father's change?" Norah asked.

Isabella dug one hand into the pocket of her

jeans. "Oh yeah. Here." She handed him a wad of crushed bills and some coins. "That's it," she said when Tom stared at the money. "Airport food equals inflated prices."

"I wasn't counting," her dad said with a chuckle. "I was just wondering how this fist-sized wad fit into the pocket of those jeans. What did you do? Have Mom sew them on you this morning?"

"Dad! They aren't that tight."

"They're pretty tight," Norah agreed. "You might wish you'd worn something more comfortable before this journey ends." She pulled at the leg of her own stretchy trousers to illustrate her point.

"Mom dresses like an old lady these days," Izzy explained to Tom as if Norah had suddenly disappeared.

Now it was Norah's turn to protest. "Isabella Wallace!"

"Well, it's true. I've been thinking of nominating you for that show where they make you throw out your entire wardrobe and go shopping for a new one."

"My clothes are fine—serviceable. Comfortable."

Izzy took another bite of her sandwich and continued to study her mother. "On that show they completely change your hair and makeup too. They can make the person look ten years younger."

Norah saw Tom mask a smile by taking a swallow of his bottled water.

"Do something. She's your daughter too."

Tom cleared his throat and spoke to Izzy while looking at Norah. "I think your mother looks—*fine,* Bella. Especially the way she's wearing her hair now—and the color—"

Norah's hand flew to her hair. "What about the color? This is my normal color. I do not—"

Tom and Isabella both burst out laughing and Norah smothered a grin. "So this is the way it's to be," she said sternly. "The two of you ganging up on poor defenseless me?"

Tom gave a hoot of laughter. "Defenseless? That'll be the day." He turned to Isabella. "One time there was this neighborhood bully. Your mother was—what, Norah? Nine—ten?"

"I was Izzy's age," Norah replied.

"But smaller than you. The bully must have easily outweighed her by fifty pounds or more. What was that kid's name, Norah?"

"Oscar," Norah said.

"So Oscar starts picking on this new kid and your mom had had it. She marched up to him, stood toe to toe between him and the new kid and told Oscar that—you finish it," Tom said, looking at Norah.

"You're telling it."

"Said what?" Isabella demanded.

Her mother sighed. "I simply informed the young man that if his name was a problem for him he should change it."

"Or words to that effect," Tom said.

"And what did Oscar do?"

"He asked me how he could change it when it was the one he was born with."

Tom took up the story. "She asked him what name he would choose for himself."

"And?" Izzy asked, glancing from one to the other. "What name?"

"Bruno!" Tom and Norah said in unison then chuckled.

Izzy took obvious delight in seeing them sharing a memory, looking at each other with no reservation, then Norah looked down and away. "And that's when you fell in love with Mom, right?"

Her father began clearing the trash from their lunch. "Uh—"

"I thought you said those paperbacks you've been reading were stories of inspiration and faith," Norah said, turning the focus on Izzy and away from her and Tom.

"Well, even God loves a good romance, Mom," Izzy replied as she took the trash from

Tom and stuffed it into the paper bag that had held the sandwiches.

"We should see if there's been any change in what's happening," Norah said and Izzy watched as her mom relieved her of the trash and they headed off in opposite directions—her to deposit their trash and him to check in with the woman at the desk. When they returned Izzy had pulled her novel out of her backpack and settled into one of the chairs.

By late afternoon Norah had called her parents and Tom had spoken to his sisters. They whiled away the endless waiting by reading, working, or—in Isabella's case—listening to music. Around five, Tom shut his laptop, stood and stretched. "Come on, girls, let's go for a walk and see about getting something hot for supper."

It had been several hours since the announcement had come through that the airport would close. Airport personnel had put the contingency plan for such situations into operation. But as night came on and the storm gathered force, it became clear that no one was going anywhere at least until morning and maybe not then.

The first thing to hit Norah as they entered the concourse was the sheer level of the noise—people shouting at each other, babies crying, toddlers and their siblings fighting in loud shrieks over some toy or snack, bleary-eyed parents slumped on the floor or on chairs ignoring their children's pleas for mediation. In spite of the fact that shopkeepers and other airport employees were as stranded as the passengers, several restaurants and shops had shut their doors. The desks at every gate stood empty of airport personnel and the arrival and departure boards had simply been turned off.

"Dad?" Isabella edged closer to Tom's side and put her hand in his. "Everybody's so mad."

Norah put her arm around Isabella's shoulder as she looked up at Tom. "This place is turning into a powder keg."

"It'll be fine. The governor has declared a state of emergency and the National Guard is handling things along with airport security."

"Still, maybe we could organize some child care. These parents need a break."

"A camp," Izzy suggested. "Camp Stuck-in-the-Snow."

"It's not a bad idea," Norah told Tom. "We could take over the play areas along the concourse—there are slides and blocks and all sorts of activities."

"And don't they have coloring books and stuff on the planes to keep the kids entertained?" Izzy asked, scooting closer to her parents so that the three of them formed a tight ring.

"We could have the kids bring their blankets and pillows for nap time," Norah said, her voice growing with enthusiasm for the idea.

Tom looked from his wife to his daughter and back to Norah. "Aren't you exhausted?"

"I could sleep," she admitted.

"But, Dad," Izzy said, "this is Mom's thing. I mean she is practically an expert when it comes to setting up stuff for helping others. Right, Mom?"

"Right." Norah raised her eyes to Tom's. "A regular wizard."

"Well, I guess it beats wearing the turkey costume I'm sure my sisters have waiting for me back home at Mom's," he said.

"Don't underestimate me," Norah told him with a shy grin. "I've been known to come up with a turkey costume myself."

Izzy threw her arms around Tom's neck and squealed, "This is such a cool adventure we're on."

Norah saw Tom glance at her over the top of their daughter's head as he said, "Yeah. Pretty cool."

On Thanksgiving morning Norah opened her eyes and blinked several times as she tried to get her bearings. Airport. Denver. Vintage military cot where she had spent a good part of the night trying to remember this wasn't even half the width of her bed at home. She grimaced as she stretched her back and legs.

"Coffee?"

Tom was standing beside her looking as if he'd just stepped out of a shower even though he was wearing the same clothes he'd worn the day before.

"Intravenously, if possible," she muttered as she struggled to a sitting position with her back against the wall. "Where's Izzy?"

"Out recruiting." At Norah's blank stare he added, "Counselors? For Camp Stuck-in-the-Snow?" Then he grinned and sat on Izzy's abandoned cot. "You never were much of a morning person, were you?"

Norah chose to ignore that as she sipped her coffee. "So what are the chances we're going to get out of here today?"

"Slim and none—take your pick. It snowed all night and hasn't let up—twenty inches and counting. Last I heard this is just the front side of an entire line of storms."

Norah groaned. "I need a shower and a toothbrush."

"Can't help with either of those. How about an

after-dinner mint?" He produced a cellophane-wrapped red-and-white candy from his pocket.

"Thank you," Norah said. As she sucked on the mint she studied him. "How come you look as if you just stepped out of *GQ* magazine or something?"

He ran one hand through his hair self-consciously. "I washed up a little."

"Tom!" A woman at the door of the club waved to him. "We're all set," she said, rushing forward and handing him a yellow legal pad with a list of names and numbers. "Every gate area has a representative."

Norah gave Tom a questioning look.

"I met with the airport manager," he said. "They thought it might be helpful to see if we could have a volunteer communicator for each gate area. Kind of cuts down on everyone trying to gain information. Also cuts down on rumors that can cause panic."

The woman had reached them now and Tom beamed at her as he took the notebook and scanned the list. "That's great work, Patty. Oh, Patty Martin, this is my—this is Norah."

Patty shook Norah's hand. She was close to forty, but with a face and body and manner of moving that made her look at least a decade younger. Norah felt old and dowdy as she accepted the woman's handshake.

"Now don't forget you promised me a ride in that sports car of yours when we get back to the world," she said turning her attention back to Tom.

The woman is flirting with my husband, Norah thought. She glanced at Tom and saw him watch the slim, fashionably dressed, perfectly made-up Patty stride back toward the door in her three-inch heels. *And he's enjoying it.*

Not your husband, she reminded herself.

"You okay?"

Tom was looking at her curiously.

"Fine," she replied tightly.

Tom sighed. "We have got to work on your vocabulary for social conversation, woman."

Woman—"my woman" he'd called her back when they were first married. "I love you, woman"—he used to say.

"I have to—" She struggled awkwardly to her feet, untangling herself from the twisted airline blanket and ignoring Tom's offered hand. She grabbed her purse and Izzy's backpack, certain that Tom would never think to keep an eye on it. He was far too busy running things, not that he'd exactly leaped on board when she'd suggested they get organized. But now that perky Patty had appeared, well—Norah headed for the women's restroom without finishing her thought.

"Hurry back," Tom called. "The gate reps can help you organize the camp."

Like I need help—is that what he thinks?

She was a mess. Her rumpled clothes screamed "slept in them" while her face was a road map of every one of her thirty-eight years. She was probably the same age as the ever-so-effervescent Patty—maybe even younger. She dug through her purse and found her hairbrush and attacked her hair with it. Then she paused and took a deep breath as she met her image in the mirror eye to eye.

Honestly, Norah Wallace, what kind of example is this to set for your daughter? There's her father out there saving the world and looking great doing it. Pull yourself together, girl. If you think he's falling into memory land with every word out of your mouth, think again. It's been five years— he's moved on and until you saw him yesterday— so had you.

Spotting Izzy's backpack, Norah rummaged through the contents, selecting items from her daughter's portable cosmetics counter and laying them out on the counter next to the sink. She opened the small tube of toothpaste that nestled with equally small bottles of lotion and founda- tion in the required plastic sandwich bag to get them past security. She squirted toothpaste onto her index finger and scrubbed her teeth. Next she smeared lotion on her face and wiped it clean with a tissue from the pack in her own purse.

Better already, she thought as she leaned toward the mirror.

This wasn't about impressing Tom or anyone else, she told herself. This was about taking pride in her appearance and setting an example for her daughter. It was about Izzy. Ever since the divorce her entire focus had been Izzy's upbringing and well-being. And just because Tom Wallace had suddenly reappeared in the flesh—in all his gorgeous, charming, glory-oozing memories she thought she had long ago laid to rest—there was no reason to start acting like a teenager with a crush.

Chapter Four

Tom did a double take when he saw Norah emerge from the restroom. Patty was introducing him to the gate reps, but Tom could not take his eyes off Norah. The cap of black curls framed her subtly made-up face. She had tucked the rumpled green T-shirt firmly into the waistband of her black slacks—slacks now belted with the long, slim scarf he'd seen Izzy stuff inside her backpack as they boarded the plane the day before. Over her shoulders Norah had tied the shapeless black sweatshirt he thought he might recognize from when they were married. Only now the contrast between the black sleeves and the green shirt highlighted her blue-green eyes, making them seem luminous. The finished look was both casual and sophisticated.

"Excuse me," Tom said to Patty and the others.

"Wow, you clean up nice," he said, moving close enough not to be heard by the others.

Norah smiled. "You know, Tom, we are really going to have to work on your compliment-giving skills," she said as she walked past him toward the group. "Hello, I'm Norah Wallace and it would be great if some of you had the time to help me organize a day camp to keep the little ones entertained until we can all get out of here."

Five or six of the reps raised their hands to volunteer.

"Excellent," Norah said. "Let's get started. Ideas?"

And with that she exited the room with her band of volunteers trailing after her. The rest of the gate reps turned their attention back to Tom and Patty.

"Okay, where were we?" Patty said. "Ah, yes, Thanksgiving dinner."

The group had finally settled into serious planning for the holiday meal when Izzy burst into the room followed by seven tall, gangly male teenagers. "Where's Mom?" she asked as soon as she spotted Tom.

"Out there organizing the day camp. I thought you were helping her."

"Oh, right," Isabella said, looking slightly abashed. "I kind of got caught up in something else."

Tom turned his attention to the young people with Bella. "Hi, I'm Bella's father, Tom Wallace."

"Oh, sorry," Isabella said as she quickly introduced the teens. "And that's Mike. They're with the basketball team I told you about?"

"Sorry about the tournament, guys," Tom said. "So what's going on?" he asked, turning his attention back to his daughter, who looked diminutive in the circle of giants.

"Well, we were talking about the day camp and you know how on the last night at summer camp we always do this talent show?" Mike explained.

Tom nodded but couldn't ignore the fact that Bella was staring at Patty. He'd seen Isabella watching him the evening before after Norah had fallen asleep, and he—restless as always these days—had taken a chair some distance from Isabella and Norah where Patty was also fighting insomnia. He and Patty had connected immediately, exchanging war stories about their high-powered careers well into the night.

New girlfriend? Isabella's look seemed to ask as she shifted her gaze to him, and for the first time since meeting Patty, Tom realized that she was a clone of every woman he'd dated and introduced Bella to over the years.

"This is Patty Martin," he said including the basketball players in his introduction. "She's the public relations director for Teen Town." That got Bella's attention. Teen Town was a popular media conglomerate with a glossy fashion magazine, a popular Web site and its own show on cable television.

"Cool," one of the giants said and the others mumbled their support.

"Bella, why don't you and your—committee— sit down with Patty here and map out a plan," Tom suggested.

Isabella frowned. "I should go help Mom."

"I'll go help your mom. This is a great idea and you and your friends are the very ones to pull it off."

As always Isabella blossomed under his praise, and he felt the familiar kick of guilt that he wasn't around to boost her confidence on a regular basis. "Okay," she said. "You're sure you'll help Mom."

Tom gave the scout's honor signal. "Promise," he said.

"Were you ever really a scout?" she asked, her eyes darting to Patty who had the entire basketball team laughing and eyeing her slim figure.

"I was not," Tom replied. He took a step closer and placed his hands on Bella's shoulders. "What I am and always will be is your father and if I make you a promise, you can count on it, okay?"

He saw from the look she gave him that they both knew he couldn't always guarantee that, but she grinned and stood on tiptoe to kiss his cheek. "She's not your type," she whispered just before she turned and hurried back to where the boys and Patty were waiting.

Tom didn't have to look far to find Norah. The woman had always been a bit of a Pied Piper when it came to getting kids to follow her lead. Her eyes sparkled as she listened to the children shout out ideas for how this day camp thing might work. An admiring group of teenaged girls and boys all dressed in matching polo shirts with the logo of their church embroidered over the one breast pocket had gathered behind Norah, no doubt awaiting their assignments. Tom took advantage of the fact that Norah had her back to him and joined the circle of teens.

"Well now, Robbie, snowball forts are a wonderful idea, but we'll have to ask the people here at the airport if that's okay."

"They've got security issues," a worldly girl of ten informed everyone.

"Exactly," Norah replied. "Now these young men and women are members of a very special choir," Norah explained, turning to indicate the teens. She spotted Tom among them and faltered.

"Is that man their leader?" a child called out.

"No," Tom replied stepping forward. "I'm Mrs. Wallace's assistant."

The children looked mystified.

"I asked them to call me by my first name," Norah explained softly. "Where's Izzy?"

"Putting together a talent show," he replied, then turned his attention back to the children. "We've got a lot of work to do, kids. Who wants to help work on the set for tonight's performance?" Tom asked.

Several of the children waved their hands and Tom selected half a dozen. "Oh, and we're going to need a stage manager," Tom said.

"Me!" The girl who had spoken earlier about airport security waggled her hand furiously at Tom.

Tom had his doubts about others being willing to follow this girl's lead. She was something of a know-it-all and in his limited experience that trait did not inspire leadership. He glanced past her hoping for more hands.

"Excellent," Norah said as she put her arm around the little girl and ushered her over to Tom. "This is Elizabeth."

"Well, Lizzie, let's—"

"It's Elizabeth," the girl informed him. "That is my name."

Tom met her look. "Elizabeth," he said solemnly. "Would you be so kind as to join the others over there?" When the girl marched off, he rolled his eyes at Norah who covered a smile as she went back to the choir practice.

The morning flew by and the children were barely aware of the continuing storm. Furthermore, with the children occupied, the adults seemed to have calmed down considerably. Norah, on the other hand, was far too focused on Tom. By the time the children's parents had come to bring lunch and help settle the younger children for their afternoon nap, it had been over an hour since she had seen Tom and his crew.

Hurrying along the concourse, she could not help but notice more changes from the previous day. One man had apparently taken it as his responsibility to walk the length of the concourse, calling out the latest weather conditions at each gate like a town crier. "Snow has stopped for now, but warming trend means sleet and icing." He just shrugged when his news was met with good-natured boos. "Don't shoot the messenger, folks."

As Norah neared the dead end of the concourse, she blinked, unable to believe what she was seeing there. The semicircular backdrop behind the desks that served the last three gates had been covered with flattened cardboard boxes cut and colored to resemble a holiday village.

Norah walked past a group of children and

adults seated cross-legged on the floor, then stopped. There in the middle of them was Tom, his fingers jammed into the child-sized handle of a pair of scissors, his tongue locked between his teeth as he concentrated on cutting a piece of folded white paper. The memory of their first Christmas in Arizona hit her like a snowball to the back of the head. Suddenly she was back in that apartment where she and Tom had first learned that she was pregnant and where her doctor had dictated no travel for her.

On Christmas Eve, devastated that they would not be in Normal for a traditional Christmas, Norah had curled up on the bed and cried herself to sleep. And when she had awakened just before midnight, Tom had been sitting on the rocking chair he'd bought her when they'd gotten the news they were pregnant. He'd been wearing one of those Santa hats available at any drugstore at that time of year, and he'd handed her a headband of reindeer antlers.

"Time to make the rounds, Rudolph," he'd said, tweaking her nose, red from crying.

She hadn't felt much like playing, but while she'd slept she'd felt worse about the fact that she wasn't the only one missing Christmas at home. How selfish was she to think only of herself when Tom was missing out as well? She'd put on the antlers and followed him into the tiny living room. At the doorway, she'd stopped and gasped for the room was lit by dozens of votive candles and a snowstorm of crudely made paper snow-flakes hung from the ceiling. In the background, the radio was tuned to an all-Christmas-music station.

"Come on," Tom had said, leading her to the loveseat he'd turned into a sleigh using the colorful fleece coverlet his mother had sent them.

"Aren't I supposed to pull the sleigh," she'd asked, indicating her antlers and red nose.

He'd grinned. "I put it on autopilot for tonight."

Together they had settled into the sleigh and sung along with the carols. Between songs, Tom had produced milk and cookies. "Perks of the job," he'd assured her, "unless you'd prefer reindeer food?"

"What's reindeer food?"

"Carrots, lettuce—healthy stuff."

Norah had curled her nose in disgust and Tom had laughed and pulled her into his arms and sung "Blue Christmas" along with Elvis as he fed her cookies.

At dawn they had exchanged gifts, but she no longer remembered what. The best gift had been Tom's re-creation of a Normal holiday. The following year, Tom had placed several sheets of white paper and a pair of scissors in front of her.

"Teach me to make a proper snowflake?" he'd asked.

And through the years of their marriage the tradition had continued—even after they'd moved into their first house and then on to the grand house that Tom had insisted on buying. And even when their arguments or stony silences had become almost an everyday occurrence—some time in December they called a truce and the tradition continued.

"Hey, Norah? Check this out."

Norah blinked, aware once again of her surroundings. Tom was holding up one perfect paper snowflake and grinning triumphantly.

By the time the sky darkened into night, pretty much everyone still confined to the concourse agreed that everything they could reasonably expect was being done to make them as comfortable as possible.

"But we can hardly be expected to ignore the future," Dave Walker, the airport director of operations, said to Tom. "The airport will reopen—possibly as early as tomorrow. My people are exhausted, too. They've been here—away from their families, I might add—for the same number of hours as everyone else. Some of them longer. Some were at the end of their shifts when this thing hit."

"We appreciate that," Tom assured him. "It's

Thanksgiving and we're just trying to make it special—for everyone."

"Still, you can't expect our vendors or the airlines to keep shelling out—"

"How about this?" Norah said. "How about if we take an offering for the meal and then divide it between the vendors according to their contribution. It might not completely pay the bill but—"

"I'll cover the difference," Tom said quietly.

Dave scratched his head and frowned. "Are you still going to want my staff to serve as waiters and—"

"No one is asking that," Norah told him. "We have volunteers ready to set up the buffet and others willing to clear away any leftovers afterward. The employees here at the airport should feel that they are as much a guest at this table as anyone else."

"Sort of like the first Thanksgiving," Tom said with a grin. "Come on, Dave, help us out here."

Dave glanced over to where the food vendors and airline managers stood. They were lined up in a show of solidarity, their arms folded across their chests. Earlier they had marched down the concourse with Dave to where Norah and Tom were setting up for the evening's meal and performance and made it clear—via Dave—that they had had it. "I'll talk to them," Dave said. "You'll pay the difference?"

Tom nodded. "I'll need receipts and invoices, but yes, tell them if they will give us access to whatever food supplies they may have on hand, they will be fully reimbursed."

Norah watched Dave approach the others. "Tom, this could be a lot of money."

Tom shrugged. "Look at these people, Norah," he said turning her away from Dave and his group to where groups of passengers were busy moving waiting-area benches into impromptu auditorium-style seating in front of the stage the children had created. "Look at their faces," he said, his hands still on her shoulders. "Close your eyes and listen."

Norah did as he asked and she heard laughter and snatches of the kind of conversation that takes place when strangers are getting to know one another. From a distant corner she heard the soft strum of a guitar and from somewhere behind her she heard the younger children busy at play in the children's area now dubbed Camp Stuck-in-the-Snow.

And through it all she was most aware of Tom's familiar strong hands resting on her shoulders, his deep quiet voice reverberating in her ear, and the rhythm of his steady breathing as predictable as her own. "We always were a good team, woman."

"Okay, you've got a deal," Dave said having returned from his huddle with the others. "Get your people organized and follow me."

Half an hour later the food started coming—an unorthodox cornucopia of hot and cold sandwiches, pizzas, oversized pretzels, prepackaged salads, single-serving containers of yogurt, fresh apples, oranges and bananas, bags of chips, pretzels and nachos, and bottled water, soda and juices. The "guests" lined up on either side of the buffet and without anyone so much as suggesting they be mindful of the numbers of people to be fed, limited their selections so there would be plenty for everyone.

"Mom, over here!"

Norah saw Isabella waving to her from the position she'd staked out near the stage. Tom was sitting on the floor next to her.

A family Thanksgiving, she thought as she made her way to them.

"Pull up a piece of floor and join us," Tom said with a grin. He started to bite into his sandwich when Isabella stopped him.

"We haven't said grace," she reminded him.

Norah could see by Tom's expression that saying grace was not exactly a regular thing for him. The truth was that if it weren't for Isabella's devout faith, saying grace probably wouldn't be a regular thing for Norah either.

"You say it, honey," she suggested.

Isabella held out one hand to either parent and

then indicated with a nod that they needed to complete this little circle by taking hands with each other. When they hesitated, Isabella sighed impatiently. "We're giving thanks," she said, "not making a lifetime commitment."

Tom laughed and grabbed Norah's hand. "Good point, Bella."

Isabella closed her eyes and bowed her head and her parents did the same. Norah could not help noticing that nearby, other small groups of passengers had observed them and paused to put down their food and join hands as well.

"Thank you, God, for this food we are so blessed to receive. Millions of people are starving tonight and we ask for your help in showing us the way to relieve such suffering even as we celebrate this day of giving thanks. Amen."

"Amen," Tom and Norah murmured together.

"That was lovely, Bella," Tom said as he released Norah's hand and leaned over to kiss his daughter's cheek. "Thank you."

"You can eat now," Bella instructed, every bit as shy about receiving a compliment as Norah had ever been.

"Kid gets more like you all the time," Tom whispered as he reached past Norah for a packet of ketchup.

"So how did we spend our first Thanksgiving

together?" Isabella asked when conversation among them faltered.

"You didn't eat much—you were still a little peanut inside Mom's tummy." Tom tweaked Isabella's nose.

"We were still in that tiny little studio apartment," Norah added and saw Tom frown.

"It wasn't that tiny." Tom had always been especially sensitive about the material environment he had provided for Norah and Isabella. Even though when they split they were living in a McMansion in a gated community with hired help to tend the grounds, the pool and clean the house, Tom had wanted more.

"Cozy," Norah amended, not wanting to open the door to old wounds and arguments. "It was our first home together."

Appeased, Tom laughed as he continued the story. "Your Mom had bought this turkey—what was it, forty pounds or something?"

Norah blushed. "Twenty," she murmured.

"Frozen," Tom added as they both started to laugh.

"And it wouldn't fit in the oven," Norah said, snorting with giggles and the memory.

"Your mom had invited the immediate world to come for dinner."

"Just a few neighbors and people from work

who had nowhere else to go that day," Norah protested.

"Twenty people in all," Tom reminded her.

"Where were you going to put them all if the apartment was so small?" Izzy asked.

"The apartment building had a flat roof," Norah explained, "so your father got this idea that we could have everyone bring lawn chairs and we'd set things up on the roof."

"Except there had been this prolonged drought and heat wave and the floor of the roof was coated with some kind of asphalt substance that not only held the heat but tended to stick to your shoes."

"But everybody was such a good sport. Remember Kyle?"

Tom grinned. "I haven't thought about Kyle in years." He turned to Isabella. "Kyle lived across the hall from us and somehow he got his hands on a child's wading pool, brought it up to the roof and filled it with ice."

"For the sodas," Izzy guessed.

"For our feet," Norah explained.

"How did you make the turkey?" Isabella asked, her eyes darting excitedly from one parent to the other.

"Mrs. Goslin," Norah said. "She was the neighbor upstairs—she seemed old then, but she couldn't have been more than—what?" Norah glanced at Tom.

"Mid- to late sixties."

"How'd she get the thing thawed in time?"

Once again Tom and Norah burst into laughter. "We ate a lot of appetizers that evening. The turkey was finally pronounced ready around— what? Nine?"

"Closer to ten," Norah confirmed. "I remember because that's about the time that her nephew— that Paul got there."

"Wait a minute," Isabella said, putting the details together. "Paul Goslin? As in the guy you went into practice with? As in the guy who sent you off to California to open a branch office?"

Tom took a swallow of his bottled iced tea. "He didn't send me, Bella. It was a great opportunity—for all of us."

"Yeah, right," Isabella muttered. "Changed our lives."

Conversation died as Isabella got to her feet. "I've got to go. It's almost time for the program to get started."

Norah half-rose to follow her, but Izzy was already gone, so she sank back to the carpet and picked at her salad.

"Sorry," Tom said.

"You still think that—you still believe that—"

She was feeling so defensive all of a sudden that it was hard to put words to her thoughts. Memories could be easy and comforting, but they could also be a reminder of harder times.

"Yeah, I still believe I was just trying to do the best I could for you and our daughter, but it's ancient history, Norah, right?"

Apparently not.

"And can you understand that I only did what I thought was best for all of us as well?"

"I guess I don't get how splitting up our family was the best thing for any of us," Tom said as he got to his feet and walked away.

Chapter Five

"Ladies and gentlemen, and boys and girls of all ages," Patty announced from the center of the makeshift stage in the voice of a circus ringmaster as soon as the dessert had been served. "It is our great pleasure to present for your entertainment this evening a program in three parts. For our opening act, may I present—" She gave a nod to one of the choir members who pounded out a drum roll on one of the gate counters, then shouted, "The kids from Camp Stuck-in-the-Snow!"

The audience applauded and cheered as the smallest of this little community of stranded souls made their way to the center of the backdrop. The children sang three numbers, their voices growing stronger and more confident with each. By the time they reached their finale—a rendition of "Let There Be Peace on Earth"—they were shouting out the words as if they wanted to be heard around the planet they sang about. As they moved into the final verse, Patty urged the audience to, "Please sing along with us."

Norah stood behind the last row of seats and watched as everyone stood and joined hands, going so far as to reach across aisles and around the ends of rows so that the chain of hands was unbroken as they belted out the chorus with the children. She felt someone move closer and take her hand and looked up to find Tom standing next to her, swaying in time to the music as he looked down at her and mouthed, "Sorry."

When the song ended there was a moment of silence and then the crowd erupted into cheers and whistles and calls for encores as the children ran off the stage to their waiting parents.

"Well, that's going to be hard to top," Patty shouted into the microphone. "But we aren't done yet. It's time for our very special version of— drum roll please! Stranded Americans with Talent!"

After the last talent act left the stage, Tom prepared to announce that a volunteer offering would be taken to help cover the costs of the meal.

"Change of plans," Dave told him. "We got together and decided nobody was out that much and we could certainly afford to donate this one meal. Take your offering, but we'd like it to be for charity."

"Thanks—thank everyone for us," Tom said as Patty handed him the microphone. He looked out over the crowd of people still buzzing from the excitement of the evening's entertainment. He gave himself a moment to soak in the sheer magic of what had happened over the last several hours. He searched the audience until he saw Norah, standing at the back with the basketball players, each of them holding one of the plastic bowls used at security checkpoints to collect loose change, watches and other small items that might set off the alarm. Tonight those bowls would be used as offering plates.

He cued the musicians and as the trio quietly played the chorus to "Let There Be Peace on Earth" Tom announced the generous gift of the airport vendors and then the collection for charity. He motioned for the church choir to take the stage and as the plastic bowls made their way up and down each row, the choir sang. By the time the last row had been served, there wasn't a dry eye in the house.

Afterward several people stayed to help reset the furnishings into the usual seating pattern at each gate. Others cleared away the remains of the food and took down the buffet tables. The teens dismantled the backdrop and stage area and by a little after ten, everything was back in its normal place as people settled in for another night.

"Have you seen Izzy?" Norah asked Tom when she found him in the airline club helping to count and record the money from the collection.

"She went off to call her friends," he said and moved away from the group, leaving them to attend to the finances. "She was pretty pumped about the evening, cheeks all rosy and eyes sparkling."

Norah tried to ignore a sense of foreboding as the two of them hurried down the concourse in the direction Tom had last seen their daughter. "It wouldn't be the first time she's lost track of time. I just hope the battery on that phone you gave her holds up."

But when Norah saw a group gathered around the entrance to the women's restroom, something told her to quicken her step.

"It's Isabella," Elizabeth's mother told her. "We just found her. She's been throwing up and—"

Tom pushed past them all. "Bella!"

Norah was close behind as Tom pounded on the locked door to the stall. Behind her she could hear people calling for a doctor. From under the stall door she could see the soles of Izzy's sneakers. Izzy heaved and heaved and between heaves, Norah could hear her shuddering sobs.

"Mommy," she called weakly.

"I'm here, baby," Norah called as she watched a frustrated and near-manic Tom decide against trying to force the door to the stall open. Instead he went to the empty stall next door, stood on the toilet seat, and stretched down to release the lock.

Oblivious to the stench and dirty floor, Norah fell to her knees beside her daughter. She held Izzy's forehead and tried to calm her. "I'm right here, Izzy. Daddy too. A doctor's coming."

Somebody thrust a package of premoistened towels toward her and blindly Norah accepted them and began wiping Izzy's mouth as she smoothed back her daughter's perspiration-soaked hair.

"Better?" she whispered when it seemed as if the nausea might have run its course.

"It hurts," Izzy moaned, cradling her stomach with her arms as she leaned back against the wall of the stall.

"I know. I know."

But Norah didn't know. She didn't know why suddenly her vibrant daughter was weak as a kitten, seemed to be running a fever and was as colorless as the towel Norah used to clean her face. She looked up and saw Tom standing in the doorway of the stall, his face almost as pale as Izzy's.

"She'll be okay," Norah promised him, but again she felt the emptiness of that vow.

"Somebody need a doctor in here?"

A man with a mass of white hair, ruddy cheeks and a neatly clipped, short white beard, eased his way past the bystanders. If he'd been wearing a red shirt he would have been a prime candidate to play Santa at the mall. As it was he was wearing wide yellow suspenders over his Oxford blue shirt.

"Ted Roth," he said, offering a handshake to Tom. "You the father?"

Tom nodded. "Are you a doctor?"

"Pediatrician." He stepped to the sink and scrubbed his hands thoroughly, then turned to the scene in the stall. "How about I take a look-see?"

He didn't wait for permission but squeezed his bulk into the tight space as Norah pulled Izzy closer.

"You look like Santa Claus," Izzy said, her voice hoarse from vomiting.

"That's the plan," Dr. Roth replied as he gently began his examination. "Helps put the kids at ease," he confided. "Is it working?"

Isabella nodded and Norah felt a little of the tension that had riveted Izzy's slim body ease away.

"When did this all start?"

"A little while ago—"

"Okay, let's see what's going on here." He gently probed her abdomen. "That tender there?"

Izzy nodded.

"How about when I stop pressing? Any pain?"

Izzy shook her head.

Dr. Roth removed a thermometer from a case he carried in his shirt pocket and shook it out. "Open," he said and placed the thermometer under Isabella's tongue. "No talking or laughing allowed," he warned as he checked her pulse against the second hand on his large Mickey Mouse watch. When Isabella started to smile weakly, he held up a warning finger. "No laughing at the doctor."

Norah saw Tom move closer. He was frowning and his hands were clenched into fists.

"Now then," Roth continued as he removed the thermometer and pushed his reading glasses into place to read it. "So let's run through this one more time." He pressed around her abdomen on her left side. "Hurt?" he asked with each probe.

Izzy shook her head.

He moved more to the right side and pressed. Izzy grimaced.

"I'll take that as affirmative."

"She had supper with us from the buffet," Norah said, trying to provide information that might prove helpful. "She had a chicken panini, carrot sticks and—"

"What was on that sandwich?"

"Chicken," Izzy replied.

Roth grinned. "You don't say." He continued examining Izzy but spoke to Norah and Tom. "I don't think it's food poisoning if that's what's coming to mind. We've got a couple of diagnostic candidates here," Roth muttered as if consulting with some invisible assistant.

"Candidates for what?" Tom asked through gritted teeth.

"Best guess without running some tests would be the appendix—assuming that organ hasn't been removed," Roth replied as he used the door to pull himself to a standing position. "Her symptoms are pretty classic, but let's not jump to conclusions until we have a little more information. The good news is that if it is her appendix, it's a relatively mild attack. No rebound tenderness."

"Meaning?" Tom asked.

"Her right lower abdomen is tender to the touch. If releasing my fingers quickly had caused an increase in pain, we'd have ourselves a situation."

Tom let out a frustrated sigh. "In English?"

"Rebound tenderness is pain that worsens when I release my hand after probing the tender area—could indicate that the infection has spread. Since Isabella isn't experiencing that, then it's likely the inflammation is localized—could heal itself with antibiotics." The doctor washed his hands again and appeared to consider several options as he dried them on a fist full of towels. "First step is to get her off that filthy floor and some place where we can make her more comfortable."

"I can't leave," Isabella protested. "I can't be away from the toilet."

"You've pretty well cleaned yourself out," Dr. Roth said kindly. "I think we can find a makeshift basin that will meet your needs."

"But," Isabella protested, then glanced up at the crowd of concerned people still crowded around and looked away. She seemed about to cry again.

"Hey, folks," Tom said, "thanks for your concern, but we've got this under control." He actually started herding people out the door who had eased their way into the bathroom. "Really appreciate everything. We'll keep you posted," he assured them and then allowed the bathroom door to swing shut.

Someone knocked lightly on the door and Tom opened it a crack as Isabella shrank farther into Norah's arms. Tom exchanged a few words with the visitor, thanked the person and when he turned back to them he was holding one of the plastic containers from security like the ones they had used as offering plates earlier.

Roth took the container and washed it thoroughly, then handed it to Isabella. "Think you can make it to your feet?"

Isabella nodded as Tom moved into position to lift and support her.

"I'll start making the arrangements to get her out of here and over to the hospital," Dr. Roth said as he extended a hand to help Norah to her feet.

"No one seems to be using the chapel," Tom said.

"Good. I'll go start putting the wheels in motion. You folks okay?"

Both Tom and Norah must have looked shocked that he could possibly think they were "okay" when Isabella was obviously so ill.

"Let me rephrase that," Roth said with a wink at Isabella. "Are you okay with getting our patient down to the chapel or should I ask somebody to bring a wheelchair?"

For an answer, Tom swept Izzy into his arms. Isabella nestled her head on Tom's shoulder and wrapped her arms around his neck.

"Mom?"

Norah was next to her in a millisecond, eager to attend to whatever need she might have. "What, baby?"

"Phone," Izzy said and nodded toward the floor of the stall they had all just vacated.

"Oh, Izzy," Norah said, but felt the first hint of a smile since the nightmare of finding her daughter sprawled on the bathroom floor had begun. She heard Tom chuckle as he shook his head and followed the doctor down the hall. Norah took the time not only to retrieve the phone and clean it off, but to also send up a silent prayer—first of thanks for sending them Dr. Roth followed by a plea that their daughter would be all right.

After Dr. Roth stopped by to assure them that he'd reached the hospital and a helicopter would be sent to transport Isabella as soon as the storm lifted.

"That could be hours," Norah objected.

"The weather reports show that the storm is almost past us. Should be able to get her moved first light. In the meantime, if she shows any signs of the pain spreading or worsening, come get me, okay?"

As Tom took his turn sitting with Isabella, he couldn't help remembering the time when he and Norah had decided to divorce. In his anger and frustration, he had wanted to—needed to—lash out and try to control the dream he felt slipping away. He had told his lawyer to demand equal custody.

Norah had been stunned. "Do you hate me so

much that you would use our child in your fight against me?"

By that stage of things they had been traveling their separate paths for months and Tom was as tired of the fight as she was. He wanted it over, but he also wanted to—needed to—win. "This is not about you," he'd told Norah, fighting to maintain calm in the face of her emotion.

"Please don't take that professional tone with me," Norah had said. "I am still your wife and this is still your daughter we are discussing."

That had brought him out of his chair and around the large ornate desk she'd bought at an antique auction for his new office when he'd made partner. "It is exactly because she is my daughter that I am doing this. You and I may not have a future together, but I will not abdicate my role as a father and surrender the total raising of Bella to you."

"Are you thinking at all about what you're asking of an eight-year-old?" Norah had shouted. "Two houses in two different states. Two different schools, teachers—sets of friends. Six months can make a huge difference in the world of children, Tom."

"Oh, come down off your social worker high horse. Bella is a people magnet. She'll make friends no matter where she is."

"I know she can do it, Tom—the question is why would we ask her to when she's not the issue."

"And you are just dying to tell me exactly what you think the issue is," he'd said, turning away from her.

She'd touched him then, her hand light on his arm, her tone gentler. "The issue is us, Tom. We find ourselves going down different paths and we're scared because we're not sure what that means, but the one thing I thought we had agreed upon was that the best thing for Izzy was to stop pretending we could work things out between us."

"I love my kid," he'd replied tightly.

"I know that and she adores you. Look, we both want the best possible life for Izzy—on that at least we are still on the same wavelength. How about this? How about you go out to California, get the office going, get yourself settled and then if you still think it's the best thing for Izzy that we share custody, I won't fight you. In the meantime, we'll go on with the original plan to alternate holidays and have her spend the summer with you."

He'd walked away from her, he remembered now and, for the first time, realized that it had not been so much wanting to turn away from her. It had been because the thing he'd wanted most was

to turn to her, to take her in his arms and beg her
to help find a way through this so they could all
be together.

Unable to sleep, Norah abandoned her cot and
collapsed onto one of the straight-backed upholstered chairs facing the small altar. It had been a
long time since she had prayed—really prayed.
Oh, she had her moments, sending hasty prayers
of gratitude heavenward when Izzy made it safely
home after being out with friends. She'd also sent
up more than her share of on-the-spot requests for
patience with her coworkers, for the energy to
keep going when her work and home life collided,
for the right words to say whenever she had to
discuss things like drugs or dating with her
growing teenager.

But truly praying as a deliberate act? She
really couldn't remember the last time. Not that
she didn't attend church. Especially since Izzy
had begun to take her faith so seriously, Norah
had been there every Sunday morning. She'd
even volunteered to help out with the youth
group. Still, religion for her—and for Tom—
had always been more of a Christmas and
Easter kind of thing. In the years before their
marriage had fallen apart, they would attend
services on the holidays and occasionally in

between—as long as it fit into their plans for the weekend.

She wondered if that had changed for Tom. She didn't think so. More than once, Izzy had returned from spending time with him and sighed dramatically at what she called his failing to understand the importance of a community of faith.

Norah folded her hands, closed her eyes and bowed her head. She waited for the words to come, but none did. Surely she shouldn't just start in begging for Izzy to be all right. And what about Izzy's idea that this entire snowstorm had been some grand plan? Ridiculous, right?

Help me understand, she prayed silently. *Show me the way—for Isabella, for myself—and yes, for what seeing Tom again after all this time means. Maybe it was just time? Or is there something I'm missing? Help me.*

Norah opened her eyes. The altar table was decorated with a Thanksgiving arrangement of flowers and produce that spilled out from a straw cornucopia over the brown linen table runner. She stared at the flowers and had the thought that while they might have been fresh a day or so earlier, they were tired-looking and beginning to fade while the produce was shriveled and dotted with the first signs of decay.

Tom sat in the chair next to her. "That flower arrangement looks like I feel," he said, his voice cracking in spite of his effort to make a joke.

Norah said nothing.

"Want me to go see if I can scrounge up something to eat or drink?" Tom asked after several seconds had passed.

"No. Thank you," Norah murmured.

Tom nodded, stood up, then sat down again, his left heel tapping steadily on the carpeted floor.

Norah placed her hand on his knee, stilling it, but she didn't look up.

"Norah?" Tom's voice was gentle and filled with concern. When she felt his hand on her shoulder and then stroking her back, she could no longer hold back the wave of fear, exhaustion and relief that Tom was at her side. But it was Tom who started to cry.

She had never felt so helpless. Her only child was lying not five feet away, curled into a fetal position, reminding her of how tiny and fragile she had seemed that day they brought her home from the hospital. Together they had placed her in the crib that Tom had spent all of one Sunday afternoon assembling for her.

Now Tom—the father of her child—was leaning forward, face in hands, sobbing as if his heart had suddenly split right down the middle.

"Hey," she said, leaning toward him as she continued massaging his back. "She's going to be fine," she added, scrambling for words that could stem the tide of his tears.

"We don't know that," he said. "You don't even believe that," he added, his voice challenging her to deny it.

"I just want to get her to a medical center where she can be checked out properly," Norah said. Sheer exhaustion swept over her in a tsunami and it was her turn to bury her head in her hands. "What if…"

"What if what?" He sat up and placed one hand on her shoulder as he swiped at his tears with the other. She wanted—needed—more. She wanted him to wrap his arms around her and tell her everything would be all right. "What if you hadn't been here?" she whispered and this time the tears were hers.

"Come here." He held out his arms and gave her the choice of accepting the comfort of his embrace or not. She wrapped her arms around him, burying her face against his shirt. "Shh," he whispered against her ear as he stroked her hair.

Eventually her sobs abated into the occasional shuddering aftermath. She felt herself go perfectly still. Was it that she had finally found a safe haven or that she had suddenly realized the position they were in? She leaned back and looked up at him. Without a second's hesitation, he bent his head to meet her upturned face and kissed her.

In an instant his kiss erased everything they'd used to build the wall between them over all these years. Even through the fog of her exhaustion, worry over Izzy and the miracle of leaning once again on Tom's strong chest and feeling his lips on hers, Norah's brain fought to sound the alarm.

Fantasy! Not real life! Danger!

But her heart beat so hard and loud that it drowned out everything but the instant memory of all the years of Tom's arms around her, his lips on hers, his body her comforter and protector against life's storms. She placed her palms on his cheeks, savored the familiarity of the stubble of his unshaven face.

And when he deepened the kiss, wrapping his arms more tightly around her as if he would never let go, Norah felt a bubble of joyous laughter replace the agony of her tears.

Oh dear heavenly Father, was this Your plan? Is it possible?

She was kissing him back when she heard a faint call.

"Daddy?"

Chapter Six

When Tom felt Norah push away from him, he suddenly remembered one night when they were teens, kissing on her parents' front porch. Norah's father had called to her from the living room and Norah had pushed Tom away and gone running for the screen door. Now it was their daughter calling out to them.

"Right here, Bella." He shielded Norah to give her the chance to regain control. Control was very important to Norah. Always had been.

Isabella squinted up at him, then cast her eyes toward her mother. "Mom?"

Norah moved quickly to Isabella's cot and knelt, her hand automatically cupping their daughter's forehead and cheeks, searching for signs of temperature change. "You slept a little," she said softly.

Isabella yawned. "I had a great dream," she said.

"Really? That's a good sign," Norah said. "What was the dream?"

Tom saw Bella glance up at him again, then back at her mother. "Nothing. You've been crying."

Norah backhanded her cheeks—dry now but her red-rimmed eyes told the story. "Yeah, well, you know me when my baby gets sick."

"Oh, Mom, I am not a baby." Isabella collapsed back onto the cot and closed her eyes. Then she sat up suddenly and grabbed blindly for the plastic bowl.

Tom joined Norah next to the cot, one hand on Isabella's back while Norah held her head over the bowl. But all that came out was a hiccup, followed by another and then another.

"Oh, honey, like you need this," Norah sympathized, but there was a little bubble of laughter underlying her words.

"It's not funny," Isabella protested between hiccups.

Tom patted her back in a motion reminiscent of burping her as a baby. "Yeah, actually it is," he said and made no effort to conceal his grin.

Isabella shot him a look of pure fury, but then she hiccupped and the three of them started to laugh.

"Well now, that sounds like things are a little

better," Dr. Roth said as he entered the chapel. "Got some news," he continued. "Your ride will be here at dawn."

"That's wonderful," Norah exclaimed, relief evident in every feature of her face.

"I've made all the arrangements for this little lady to be checked out as soon as we reach the hospital. If as I suspect we can treat this thing with antibiotics, then you folks can take her home and work with your own doctor."

"Thank you," Norah said.

"But if the appendix needs to come out?" Tom asked.

"We're ready to handle that at the hospital. Let's just see how it goes—Prepare but Don't Project has always been my motto." He turned his attention to Isabella. "Think you can hang in there for another hour or so, young lady?"

Isabella nodded.

After the doctor left, Tom watched Norah focus all of her attention on Isabella. They had kissed and she was acting as if nothing had happened. Worse. She was acting as if kissing him had been a mistake.

"I'm going to get my laptop. You need anything?"

"No. Thanks," Norah replied, her voice lowered to a whisper as Isabella fell almost instantly asleep. "You go ahead. We'll be fine here."

"I'm coming back," Tom said, fighting to keep the edge from his voice.

"There's really no need," Norah said.

"She's my daughter too, Norah."

Finally she looked at him. Her eyes were wide and her mouth was drawn into a pucker of surprise. "Of course she is, Tom. I just thought—I just—"

Tom turned on his heel and wrenched open the chapel door. "I'll be back," he muttered and pulled the door closed behind him with a firm click.

The concourse was quiet. Here and there a few people were still awake, reading or talking softly. The televisions in each gate area had been muted so that breaking news was still immediate but without the intrusive sound of the talking heads.

Tom entered the lounge and headed to the corner where they'd spent the night before. Across the room Patty Martin's manicured nails clicked away at her computer keyboard. She glanced up and raised an eyebrow.

"She'll be fine," Tom mouthed, but made no effort to go over and fill her in on the details. He was well aware that Patty Martin was attracted to him. He was also aware that she was a bright, energetic and good-looking woman. Under other circumstances—like two days earlier—he would have considered getting to know her better. But now when he looked at her, he couldn't seem to stop comparing her to Norah.

Who was he kidding? He couldn't stop thinking about kissing Norah, having her back in his arms. Being together again—the three of them like old times. Better times.

Clearly the kiss hadn't meant that much to her. She'd practically dismissed him. He should stay here while she kept watch? Why not both keep watch? Why mightn't Bella need him as much as she might need Norah if she took a turn for the worse before they could get her out of here? And what if Norah needed him as she had earlier? No one could convince him that she hadn't made a conscious decision to come into his arms, to kiss him. She might regret it now, but if Bella hadn't called out, what might have happened?

Norah was still trying to work through Tom's earlier reaction when he returned. He stopped next to Isabella's cot.

"How's she doing?"

"A little better, I think."

Tom moved to a far corner of the chapel and unpacked his laptop. "Are you going to work?" Norah asked, trying to smooth the awkwardness between them.

"I'm going to see if I can get flights out of here

after Bella is checked out at the hospital. I'm assuming you want to head back to Phoenix instead of continuing on to Normal?"

Norah was confused. He was being so formal, so overly polite. History had taught her that both were symptoms that Tom was upset about something.

"Norah?"

She tried to decipher what could be seething beneath his calm exterior. "Yeah. I have to be at work Monday morning and by the time we actually make it to Mom's we'd practically have to turn right around and start for home and with Izzy not—"

"Okay," Tom said and began tapping information into the computer.

Okay? Norah thought as she watched him. *What is going on here? It's the kiss. He regrets the kiss and now he's embarrassed. He always got angry whenever he was embarrassed or whenever he made a mistake.* Norah felt her own prickle of irritation. *Maybe I regretted the kiss as well. Did you ever think of that, Thomas Wallace?*

"There's a commuter flight from Denver to Phoenix at seven on Saturday morning. Assuming they get the runways cleared and traffic moving that's probably your best bet."

"Saturday?"

Tom could not let out an exasperated sigh. "It's the best choice, Norah. By the time we get Bella to and from the hospital—assuming there's no need for her to actually be admitted—it's going to be late. Traffic will just be starting to get untangled. Flights out of here tomorrow are going to be jammed and—"

"Don't lecture me, Tom. I understand the logistics. I was simply repeating the day." Norah forced herself to remain calm and took some pleasure in the fact that Tom clearly noticed the difference.

In the old days whenever they had an argument, Norah would shout at him, instantly certain that somehow he was accusing or blaming her.

"So should I book the flight?"

"Please," Norah said, reaching for her purse. "I'll get you my credit card number."

"I'll use mine."

"Tom, I—"

"Just stop it, Norah. I want to get her home as much as you do."

"Stop what?"

"Stop trying to do everything by the book—by the rules we set up five years ago. You pay for this and I pay for that. Well, I want to do this for my daughter and—"

"*Our* daughter," Norah corrected as she folded her arms across her chest to hide her clenched fists.

Tom looked down at the keyboard. "You know what I'm saying, Norah." He completed the online transaction, then took out a yellow legal pad from his briefcase and scrawled some numbers on the top sheet. "This is your confirmation number and e-ticket numbers," he said as he tore off the sheet and handed it to her.

"Thank you," Norah said primly as she folded the paper in quarters. She was going to put the paper in her purse, but hesitated. "Tom?"

He gave her that half look that he used to think passed for attention whenever he was working and she wanted to talk about something important.

"Look at me," she whispered.

He looked down first, then closed the cover of the laptop and set it aside. He placed the palms of his hands on his knees and finally raised his eyes to her—without really raising his head.

Aware that Isabella was sleeping only a few feet away, Norah pulled one of the upholstered chapel chairs close to Tom and sat knee to knee with him.

"Look, everything about these last two days has been surreal," she began, keeping her voice low.

To her relief Tom visibly relaxed slightly. "You could say that."

"And neither one of us has had a lot of rest and

then there was the excitement of the Thanksgiving program and then Izzy getting so sick."

Tom nodded as she ticked off each item. He was looking at the floor now and she almost didn't hear him mumble, "I never want to be that scared about Bella again."

"I know," she whispered. "And the worst part is, I mean, even if it does turn out that she needs to have her appendix removed, it could have been something so much worse."

"Yeah."

"I was thinking about all of that earlier," Norah continued. "Sometimes it hits me out of the blue—I mean how helpless I really am to protect her from everything that could happen."

"Me, too," Tom said. "Sometimes I just want to put her inside some kind of magical bubble where nothing can ever hurt her."

"When we saw her lying there, so sick and miserable, I was so—grateful—that you were here. That I wasn't facing this alone."

Tom glanced up and then back at his hands. "I'm always here, Norah, for whatever Bella needs."

And me? Norah thought and quickly stuffed that selfish need back inside as she had for years. "Hey, what I'm trying to get to here is that earlier—when I fell apart—" She swallowed.

"When we kissed?" Tom asked, his eyes meeting

hers directly now, holding her there, each of them unable to look away. "Is that what you're trying to say, Norah?"

"Yes," she whispered. "I just didn't want you to think that—I mean, it was a moment—a wonderful moment—but I just—"

Tom stared at her for a long moment and then to her surprise he stood up. "I know. Don't sweat it, okay? We both were overwrought with worry and exhaustion." He stretched. "I'm beat and you must be exhausted. How about you get some rest?" He started arranging chairs into a makeshift bed. "You can lie down here." He handed her a blanket he'd brought from the club.

Norah stood as well. "There's no reason we can't both get some rest. That is if you'll stop being so cavalier about this whole thing."

This whole thing? Was she talking about getting through the night or was she still on the kiss? Norah really didn't want to think about the answer to that question.

"Fine," Tom said and kicked off his shoes as he settled onto the four chairs he'd lined up.

Fine, Norah thought. They were right back where they'd started.

Friday morning dawned clear and sunny and the public address system woke anyone still sleeping with the news that the airport would reopen as soon as at least one runway could be cleared. A cheer echoed up and down the concourse.

"So, what's the plan?" Isabella asked, her voice thick with sleep.

"Well, first we're going to the hospital to be sure you're really all right," Norah said as she bustled around realigning chairs in rows and folding the blankets she and Izzy had used.

"I feel okay," Izzy protested.

"Nevertheless, Dr. Roth—"

"Aka Saint Nick," Isabella said with a grin.

"He's made all the arrangements and we're going to the hospital."

"Where's Dad?"

"I don't know. Probably washing up or making arrangements for you and me to get back to Phoenix."

Izzy's eyes widened. "You mean we're not going to Wisconsin after all?"

"We need to get you home."

"You mean, you have to get back so you can be at work Monday."

"That's not fair, Izzy. Assuming you don't need surgery to remove your appendix right away, we need to find out what's happening and how to watch for symptoms."

Isabella frowned and refused to meet Norah's pointed look. She tried getting up only to sit down immediately. "Whoa," she whispered.

"Are you dizzy?"

"Just a little lightheaded," Isabella admitted. "I'll be fine. Really, Mom, just help me change and fix my hair. I can't let anybody see me like this—especially after last night." She moaned. "That was so embarrassing."

The door to the chapel opened. "Is there a princess in here?" Tom called as he wheeled a chair into the room. "Oh, you must be the Princess Bella," he said. "I have your chariot, Your Highness, and your public awaits."

"I am not leaving this chapel until I've made myself look at least halfway decent."

Tom frowned. "Gee, that could take some time," he said, shaking his head sadly as he looked pointedly at her rumpled clothing and tangled hair. "On the other hand, I see you have called upon your fairy godmother here to work her magic. Good luck," he said winking at Norah.

We're okay, she thought with relief. *Everything's going to be okay.*

"You just step outside and guard the door," she instructed Tom. "You'll see what a hairbrush and a touch of lipstick can do."

Tom did as she asked but periodically opened

the door a crack and called in comments. "Any-thing yet?"

"Daddy!" Isabella would squeal each time and Norah would just laugh. It felt so good to be getting back to normal. Already Norah was thinking ahead. It was a habit she'd developed after Tom left. Always trying to second guess what might come up. If God had a plan, then Norah was sure she under-stood it. Now that the ice of a five-year separation had been broken, they could go their separate ways. Only now she could imagine many times like this—times they would share as Isabella's parents—and as the good friends they had always been.

"Mom?"

Norah continued brushing Izzy's hair, scooping it into the high ponytail she preferred and anchor-ing it with a wide barrette. "Hmm?"

"You know that dream I mentioned?"

"Tell me," Norah said as she watched her daughter apply lip gloss like a professional.

"I dreamed you and Dad kissed."

"Really?" Norah heard her voice crack. Izzy had seen them after all.

"It wasn't a dream, was it?" Izzy asked quietly.

Norah sat next to her and pulled Izzy into a hug. "No, but honey, it's also not what you think."

"You still love him," Izzy said, her voice muffled against Norah's neck.

Norah gently took Isabella's shoulders and held her so that they were face-to-face. "I know you don't want to hear this, but one day when you're older—"

Isabella grimaced. "Not the 'when you're older' speech."

"Someday when you're older you'll understand that it is indeed possible to love someone even though the two of you have gone down different paths. Daddy and I love you and because of that shared love for you, we will always respect and care for each other."

Isabella pulled away and flung herself into the wheelchair. "Keep on telling yourself that, Mom." She grabbed her phone. "The princess is ready!" she bellowed toward the door as she checked for messages.

But the scene that greeted Norah and Isabella outside the chapel was enough to make Isabella forget all about connecting with her friends back home. As Tom wheeled her through the double chapel doors a chorus of applause, whistles and cheers greeted her. The members of the church choir and the basketball team were there, as were several of the younger children and their parents. In a flurry of handshakes and hugs the other teens said their goodbyes and promised to stay in touch.

"Where's Dr. Santa Claus?" Isabella asked, her good spirits restored.

"He's waiting with the helicopter team."

"Like one of those flight for life things?" Isabella said. "Hey, I feel fine—well, a lot better," Isabella assured them. "Let's just stay here. We'll miss our flight to Chicago."

"We're not going to Chicago, honey. Remember?" Norah explained as Tom navigated his way through a door marked Employees Only and down a ramp.

Isabella's face tightened into the same "I'm not happy" expression she had used to good advantage since she was two. "I don't see why not."

"Because it is already Friday. The chances of our getting a flight out today are not that good and even if we did, this weather is moving toward Chicago. Dad has already made arrangements for a flight back to Phoenix tomorrow."

"You know that place you work can operate without you," Isabella said, every syllable a challenge to Norah to deny it.

"And they will if I can't be there." She turned to Tom to explain. "We're meeting with this major foundation on Monday to make our presentation for some key funding. Without it—"

Tom nodded sympathetically.

"When it comes to putting your job ahead of

everything—and everyone—else, you're as bad as he is," Isabella announced, folding her arms tightly across her chest.

"That's uncalled for," Tom said. "Apologize to your mother."

"Sorry," Izzy muttered.

Norah met Tom's look and shrugged.

As promised, Dr. Roth was waiting for them on board the helicopter. "How do you like my sleigh?" he joked.

"Pretty twenty-first century," Isabella assured him.

When they arrived at the hospital, Isabella was whisked off for blood tests, an abdominal X ray and ultrasound. "Looks to me like you dodged a bullet this time," Dr. Roth announced later after he'd gotten all the results.

"We can go home?" Norah asked.

"Just in time to get back to school bright and early Monday morning."

Isabella did not see the humor in that. "We're supposed to be on our way to see my grands—both sets," she said with an accusing look at Norah.

"Well now, you still need to take things a little easy," Roth replied and Norah could see that he had taken in the tension radiating between mother and daughter. He wrote out a prescription for anti- biotics and handed it to Tom. "You can get that filled in the hospital pharmacy," he said, then turned his attention back to Isabella. "Frankly, I'd rather see you back at home where you can get to your own doctor if these horse pills don't work."

Izzy rolled her eyes. "Boy, you grown-ups do stick together, don't you?"

"Isabella!" Tom said, his voice soft but no less of a warning.

"Sorry."

"No harm. Lots of folks had their plans spoiled, I expect," Roth said cheerfully. "On the other hand, you and your folks here sure made a difference. You should take some pride in that."

Norah saw Izzy's bad mood start to crack at the edges. "Everybody pitched in," she said, but it was clear that she had absorbed the doctor's praise.

"That's the way of it," Roth said. "Someone steps up to lead and then others fall into line and before you know it, you've got something." He studied the final test results the nurse had just brought him.

"Well?" Tom asked.

"Everything looks good," Roth said, then helped Izzy down from the examining table. "Sorry I can't offer my sleigh to get you back to the airport."

"That's okay," Isabella replied.

Tom shook Dr. Roth's hand. "Thanks for everything, doc."

Roth accepted the gratitude, then turned his attention to Norah. "You're looking a little peaked, Mom. How about letting Dad here take the first shift once the three of you get home while you get some rest?"

The three members of the Wallace family froze. Isabella recovered first. "They don't—we live in Phoenix and Dad's in—"

"Oh, well, then, my prescription is for *both* of you ladies to get as much rest as possible over the next couple of days. Can't have Mom coming down with something now that you're on the mend, can we?" He put his arm around Isabella's shoulder and walked her to the door.

They stopped by the pharmacy on their way to the exit where the town car Tom had hired waited. Dr. Roth hugged Isabella again, then held his arms open to Norah. An invitation Norah found herself accepting as if her own father had suddenly appeared and offered her the comfort she needed. Her eyes welled with tears as she blubbered her thanks.

"Now then, everything's going to work out," Roth promised and while Norah understood he was speaking in terms of the medical situation, she had a moment's fantasy that perhaps he had seen into the future and was assuring her about that.

"I can't imagine what's got into me," she said

as she stepped away from the doctor and saw Tom watching her closely.

"You're exhausted and it's been a grueling couple of days," Roth replied. "Get some rest and make sure she takes those pills—all of them even if she's feeling better. Doctor's orders."

Norah nodded and followed Izzy into the backseat of the car, while Tom went around to the passenger side. By the time they reached the airport, Tom had completed arrangements for changing flights for Norah and Isabella so they would be home as quickly as possible.

"Are you still going to Normal?" Isabella asked as Tom walked them to their gate the following morning.

"No. Hey, how about you and I go for Christmas—a good old-fashioned Wisconsin white Christmas?"

Isabella wrinkled her nose. "Actually I've about had it with the snow thing," she admitted. "Hawaii sounds good all of a sudden—or how about Cancún?"

Tom laughed. "Now what would you know about Cancún?"

"I know it has beaches and beautiful sunny weather," Bella replied. "Not to mention boys— *cute* boys."

"Give the Wisconsin idea some thought," Tom said as he kissed her forehead and handed her the backpack he'd been carrying for her. "We are not going to Cancún—at least not until you're several years older."

"That's our zone," Norah said as the gate agent called for passengers to board. She took her time gathering the last of their things, shy now that the moment of departure was actually at hand.

"You were terrific, Norah—with everyone," Tom said in a voice that was false and overly hearty.

So that's how we'll play this, Norah thought. She turned and gave him a bright smile. "Don't be a stranger," she said gaily as she started edging toward the jetway door along with dozens of other passengers.

Tom frowned. "Five years wasn't my idea," he said softly, his eyes riveted on hers, daring her to look away.

Instead she laughed nervously. "Well, no but it wasn't a contest, Tom. I mean neither one of us— either one of us could—"

They were at the doorway. Norah fumbled for their boarding passes and when she looked up, Tom was giving Isabella a final hug. Norah froze, remembering his arms around her the evening before, remembering his kiss, remembering…the feeling of having come home at last.

"Ma'am?"

Norah opened her eyes and saw the gate agent leaning toward her, a concerned look on her face. "You need to board now," she said gently, as if talking to a passenger who just might be a problem.

Norah nodded and stepped back to allow Izzy to head down the long hallway ahead of her.

"Norah?"

When she turned, Tom was standing at the door. "Call me when you get home," he mouthed.

Norah nodded and swallowed another wave of emotion similar to the one that had hit her when Dr. Roth hugged her. *Admit it,* she ordered herself as she made her way past passengers jockeying for overhead bin space to where Izzy was already curled up in the window seat, her head resting against the window and her eyes closed. *Dr. Roth was right. It's been an emotional roller coaster these last two days. Time to get back to normal— not the town—the status.*

"Izzy?"

The teenager frowned but did not open her eyes.

"Are you feeling all right?"

"Physically, yes," she replied tersely.

"Well, at the moment, that's the important thing," Norah replied.

Izzy's eyes flew open. "Oh, you mean my emotional and mental health don't count?"

Now it was Norah's turn to sigh. She simply was too exhausted to deal with teenaged drama at the moment. "Of course they count, Isabella. But right now, could we just concentrate on getting home? I promise you we can have a long discussion about anything you like once we've accomplished that."

"Whatever." Isabella twisted in her seat and closed her eyes again as Norah smiled up at the elderly woman about to take the aisle seat.

Chapter Seven

First thing Monday morning Norah took Isabella to the pediatrician. After a second round of tests and a thorough examination the doctor recommended waiting before going ahead with surgery. "It could be years before she has another flare-up and you never want to subject a patient to surgery—even routine surgery—unless it's absolutely necessary."

She had delivered this recommendation in her office with Norah and Izzy sitting across from her and Tom on speakerphone.

Norah could tell by the extent of Tom's questions that he was not convinced and she completely understood why the doctor suggested they might want to get a second opinion. "But after talking things over with Dr. Roth, the two of us concur that surgery at this point just is not indicated."

"So, Dad, technically we've got a second opinion," Isabella said. "I'm fine. Really. Okay?"

Tom finally agreed to the doctor's suggestion that Isabella come in for regular checkups over the next several months. "If there is any change—any new flare-up," the doctor assured him, "we'll take immediate action."

"Dad," Isabella begged.

"Sounds like a plan," Tom said finally. "Norah? Could you be sure an appointment gets scheduled right before Christmas so when Bella is out here—"

"I'll take care of it," Norah promised.

And while Isabella's physical health had definitely improved by the time she returned to school after the appointment on Monday, her disposition had not.

"We could *all* spend Christmas in Normal," she suggested that night at supper.

"It's your time with Dad," Norah reminded her.

"Yeah? So?"

Norah sighed. "Honey, stop matchmaking."

"Somebody has to," Izzy grumbled as she left the table and stormed off to her room. "Because you and Dad are beyond hopeless," she shouted just before the door slammed.

For the remainder of the week they coexisted in a state of silent tension. Norah because she had so much work to catch up on and the presentation on Monday had not gone well. Izzy because she'd bought into the fantasy created by their adventure in Denver and now had to come to terms with the reality of their situation.

Norah's commute to work was half an hour at best in the off-season. Once the snowbirds arrived—and more often than not they came as early as November these days—the commute was doubled. That meant that depending on how her day went, it could be seven o'clock before she made it home. The minute she entered the offices of the White Horse Social Services Agency on Friday morning, she knew this was going to be one of those days.

"Staff meeting at ten," Abby Driscoll said as she hurried down the hall and out to her car. "If I'm not back, take good notes."

Norah watched Abby, marveling at the young woman's ability to navigate on the stiletto heels she insisted on wearing. Norah had to wonder if she had ever been that young, that sure of herself. She shook her head and headed for her cubicle where the message lights on both her phone and her computer were blinking. Five calls and several dozen e-mail responses later, she picked up her notebook and headed down the hall for the staff meeting.

To her surprise everyone else—including Abby—had arrived ahead of her. Their faces told the story.

"We didn't get the grant," Norah guessed. Her heart sank. When they'd completed the presentation on Monday, the foundation's representatives had responded with only polite interest.

"Same story," Luke Randolph said, speaking to the entire group. "As long as there's gambling on the reservation, it doesn't matter how strong our business plan—no foundation is going to fund the program."

"But it's exactly because we don't want to use the profits from gambling—it's because some of the very people most in need of our services have been wiped out by their addiction to gambling, it's because—" Norah could not seem to stem the tidal wave of her protest.

Luke held up one hand to stop her. "We are all frustrated and disappointed, Norah. Still the facts are there—have always been there. Outsiders believe that with all the profits the nation earns through the casino, we shouldn't need money. We just need to find another way."

"In the meantime, we've got bills and we've put off paying them waiting for this funding," the finance manager reminded them.

"For now the program goes on hold until we

can get back on firm financial ground." Then
Luke pounded the table firmly with the side of
one fist. "This is a good program," he said, his
voice rising. Everyone on the small staff knew
that voice. It was his "pulpit" voice. Before re-
placing Norah's friend and mentor, Dr. Stan
Morrison, as head of the agency, Luke had been
a lay minister and this was the voice he'd used to
spur his congregation to action. "Let's all take the
day to think and consider alone and then come
together here at four to brainstorm new ideas."

As chairs scraped against the worn linoleum
floor, Norah gathered her notebook and pen and
prepared to follow the others back to their cubicles.

"Norah, could you stay a moment please?"
Luke was looking down at his clipboard—his
blank clipboard, meaning he was avoiding looking
at her.

They had a brief but sticky history—she and
Luke. Shortly after coming to the agency, he'd
asked her out for coffee, telling her that he needed
to be brought up to speed on the agency's history
and mission and Stan had suggested he talk to
Norah. Somehow the talk had turned to their
personal lives—her divorce, the end of a long-
term romantic relationship for him.

Over the next several weeks Luke surprised
her by stopping by the house unexpectedly—

originally with the pretense of something related to work, but after a couple of weeks just showing up unannounced. Norah had been flattered. Luke was handsome and charming. He showed an interest in Isabella and her activities. He began coming to their church, slipping into the pew next to Norah and Isabella. There had been kisses and one very uncomfortable grappling session in his car after he'd brought Norah home one night.

Luke had told her of his grandiose plans for the agency and he had persuaded Norah to abandon her fieldwork in favor of becoming the agency's full-time fund-raiser and grant writer. That's when he'd hired Abby—and in time he'd stopped dropping by, taking Norah on dates, and coming to church—at least her church.

She sank back into her chair as Luke moved to close the door behind the others. "I'll call Carol Williams—the foundation director." Action was Norah's immediate response to any sign of trouble. "Maybe if I—"

Luke took his time pulling out the chair across from her and pulling his clipboard and pen over to his new position. "Whatever happens, Norah, you know better than anyone here that we have to make some cuts—at least in the short-term. Once we find the funding, it would be my hope that we could return to full staffing, but for now—"

"You're firing me?"

"We've exhausted all reasonable possibilities for getting a grant, Norah. You've written brilliant proposals, but surely you must understand that the agency cannot afford a full-time person to write grants."

"I thought I was the agency's fund-raiser, that grant writing was just one of my responsibilities. Are you saying you no longer need to raise funds to sustain the work?" Norah forced herself to maintain a tone of calm and reason that she was far from feeling.

"Of course not, but—"

"Luke, you asked me to take this position—to give up my fieldwork. I can understand revising staff responsibilities, but surely you don't plan to simply abandon the program for families and individuals affected by gambling addiction. Put me back in the field. I can still offer counseling and—"

"And what would Abby do?" Luke asked. "She's the mother—the single mother of three small children, Norah—"

"I'm a single mother," Norah reminded him.

Luke smiled. "I know, but you have far more resources than Abby—a master's degree in social work for starters and an impressive résumé. Finding another position will be far more likely for you than Abby, with her bachelor's and the fact that this is her first job. Besides, your daughter is older and you've mentioned how supportive her father is—financially as well as emotionally. Abby has no one."

How dare you use what I told you in confidence against me? How dare you play on my friendship with Abby and my sympathies for her situation?

"Shouldn't any change in my position here relate to the performance of that work?" Norah reminded him.

Luke frowned. "I'm asking you to do what's necessary to make sure the work you've helped us do can continue, Norah. This isn't easy for me, you know. You've been here right from the beginning. I value your friendship, your contributions, your—"

I need this job but I will not beg you for anything, Norah thought. She closed her eyes. Suddenly she found herself thinking of how Tom might handle such a situation. *If you know you're right, then fight.*

"So let me be clear about this," she began, knowing from all the times she and Tom had argued that his first ploy was always to lay out the facts. "You find no fault with the work I've done here?"

"This is purely a strategic move to save the agency. Once we are on solid footing again I— we would be thrilled to have you come back."

"And earlier you instructed the staff—myself included—to take the day to come up with ideas for regaining that footing?"

Luke looked away.

"But now you are in fact making decisions without allowing me the same opportunity you're willing to offer every other staffer all of whom joined the agency after I did?"

"Well, now—"

Norah stood. "I deserve that opportunity, Luke, and unless you want to find yourself—and the hiring and firing practices of this agency—under scrutiny by the media, I suggest that you wait until after our meeting at four to fire me."

Luke stood as well. "Don't threaten me, Norah."

"That wasn't a threat, Luke. That was a promise. I'll see you at four."

When she left the conference room, the others peered at her over the low walls of their cubicles. A moment after she sat down at her desk, Norah could hear keys tapping all around her and knew the e-mails were flying back and forth along with speculation about the future—hers and the agency's.

She looked down at her own hands and knotted them into fists to stop them from shaking. Her heart hammered as she realized that she had probably just sealed her fate. *Not without a fight,* she thought and reached for the phone.

Her first call was to Carol Williams. Without asking for specifics on why the foundation turned them down, she asked Carol for tips they might use as they approached other funding sources. And with Carol's permission she recorded every suggestion—even though there was little in what she heard that they didn't already know. On the other hand, Norah had the feeling Carol was holding back.

Next she typed up a transcript of Carol's comments and forwarded it to the other members of the staff with a note saying that this information might provide some valuable insights as they thought about possible direction for the future. She copied the e-mail to Luke. Almost immediately she hit the link to compose another e-mail and typed in Tom's address, then stopped.

What was that about? She hadn't contacted Tom for advice about her job in all the time they'd been apart. Why now?

She cancelled the message and instead called a neighbor to ask her to let Izzy stay there until Norah finished work. Next, she left a message on Izzy's cell phone with instructions to go home with her friend, MJ. Then she absently fingered the phone keypad, tapping in eight of the ten numbers needed to reach Tom before she put her phone on voice mail, grabbed her sunglasses and headed for the door. "I'm going for a walk," she said. "I'll be back for the meeting at four."

She walked to the trailhead behind the agency and began hiking up the path. When she reached the top, she sat on a large boulder that overlooked the valley below. *Please help me know the right thing to say and do,* she prayed silently. *I am so unsure of how things are going. Everything about my life seems to be topsy-turvy all of a sudden. Izzy is still upset about there being no complete reconciliation between me and Tom and if I'm completely honest with myself, I admit that I bought into the fantasy myself. Now my job is in jeopardy. Not questioning Your plan, just need to know what You want of me.*

"Help," she whispered aloud as she looked up at the line of clouds gathering on the horizon. Then she pushed herself to her feet and trudged back down the path. But when she reached the office, the others told her that Luke had left shortly after she did with no explanation. He'd gotten a phone call that seemed to upset him and rushed off. In answer to their question about rescheduling the meeting, he'd told them Norah would handle rescheduling the meeting.

"Well, since I assume we've all made arrangements to stay late tonight, I see no reason why we shouldn't go forward," she said. "We can brainstorm, build a plan of action and give our report to Luke when he returns."

Tom stared at the computer screen. He'd finally wrapped up the Osbourn project, but now there were several new—and equally complex—cases in need of his attention. He glanced at the clock. Midnight.

There had been a time when the challenge of his work had energized rather than exhausted him. But ever since he'd returned from Denver… He flipped open his cell. No messages. He scrolled down the numbers and stopped on Norah's.

He put down the phone, surprised that he'd even reached for it in the first place. And where had that thought come from? He hadn't been thinking of Norah and certainly would never call her at such a late hour. It was Bella he was concerned about. Bella he had called daily or Norah he'd phoned two or three times to check on Bella's health in the two weeks he'd been back.

He forced his attention back to the computer screen. Ten minutes later he felt his cell vibrate against his hip. He flipped open the lid. *Norah?*

It was one o'clock in the morning in Phoenix. This could only be bad news.

"Norah?"

"Oh, Tom, hi. I thought you'd be asleep, so I was going to just leave you a message. I mean—it's—"

"Is it Bella?" Tom felt his heart hammer as he relived the moment when he had first seen his daughter pale and limp on the airport restroom floor.

"No—well, yes. I mean it's not what you think. Physically she's fine."

"But?"

"I don't know—you know teenagers. Their mood swings can be hard to track. She's barely speaking to me and then when I got home from work today, she was filled with news about this 'life satisfaction and outlook' survey she'd seen in some magazine. She left it out for me to complete."

"Maybe I should take that survey," Tom said and then wondered why. He had exceeded his wildest expectations when it came to achieving the career goals he'd set for himself. He had a beautiful daughter who was kind and loving and seemed to have inherited some of his flair for leadership. An ex-wife who had embraced the idea of a parenting partnership. He—

"Tom?" Norah's soft voice brought him back to the conversation at hand. "There is one thing that worries me."

"What?"

"Well, ever since we came home from the

Thanksgiving fiasco, Izzy has—I don't know. It's like she's pulling away—not just from me but everything."

"She's probably still getting her bearings. She was pretty sick and that's got to have taken a lot out of her. Maybe it's just an energy thing."

"No," Norah said. "I can't put my finger on it, but there's a definite shift in her attitude."

"Toward you?"

"Me, her schoolwork, everything. Remember how excited she was about all her activities at the church?"

Tom chuckled. "Yeah. There was a point there when I thought she was going to tell me that she wanted to be a minister when she grew up."

"She did," Norah said. "That's just it. I used to have to practically drag her out of there on Sundays and it was imperative that we arrive at least half an hour before Sunday School started. These last couple of Sundays I've had trouble just getting her out of bed."

"Have you asked her what's going on?" Tom had not achieved the success he enjoyed by beating around the bush. Norah, on the other hand, had always been overly sensitive—in his opinion—about not upsetting other people.

"Of course I've asked," Norah snapped.

"And?"

"And either I get the fake smile and the wide eyes and something along the lines of, 'I've just got so much on my plate right now,' or I get the scowl and the silent treatment punctuated by dramatic sighs."

"Do you want me to talk to her?"

Norah paused for longer than was normal for a phone conversation as if she were wrestling with her decision. Finally she let out a long breath. "No, that might just make things worse. Thanks and thanks for listening. It helps. This is ridiculous. I shouldn't have called—now there will be two of us not sleeping."

"I wasn't sleeping, Norah, and I can do more than listen," Tom said. "I am her father."

"Maybe when she's with you for Christmas, you can see what you think—see if you notice any change. I'm probably just overreacting."

"Speaking of Christmas, the more I think about it, the more I think Bella and I should forget Hawaii and go to Wisconsin. What do you think—I mean, about going? The three of us? It might be a chance for us to both talk to Bella— present a united front."

Another long silence. Tom tried to imagine Norah's face, the way she was probably curled into a corner of the sofa, her bare feet tucked under her, one finger tracing the pattern of her nightgown.

"I don't think that's a good idea."

This time Tom sighed—in exasperation. "Please don't tell me it's going to be another five years before you're comfortable being in the same place with me, Norah."

"This isn't about you," she replied, her voice edged with defensive irritation. "This is about what's best for Izzy—it's always been about that and you know it."

"And the problem with our daughter being able to actually have both her parents on site for a major holiday along with all four grandparents who aren't getting any younger would be?"

"Oh, Tom, don't play dumb. You know what she wants—what she's always hoped would happen." Then he heard her breath catch and very softly, almost inaudibly, she whispered, "That's it."

"What?"

"Remember when we were in Denver?"

"Hard to forget."

"Well, everyone was making the best of it, but Izzy was relishing the entire situation. Think about it. She was settling in—making friends and organizing talent shows and in between she was making sure the three of us ate together and caught up at the end of the day before we went to sleep. She was pretending we were a family, Tom."

"I don't know. She's pretty savvy, don't you think?"

"She is, but remember—she even suggested that the blizzard was part of God's plan?"

"Yeah, but—"

"She wasn't talking about God's grand plan for the universe, Tom. She truly believed that God put us all there and sent the storm to keep us there so we could become a family again."

"Oh, come on, Norah. That's pretty far-fetched even for a thirteen-year-old's imagination."

"No. You didn't see her in the weeks right after she joined the church, Tom."

Because I was working—at some conference in Europe, Tom thought and felt the stab of guilt that had been his constant companion during that trip.

"She was inspired," Norah continued. "It was like she'd gotten some grand new insight into life. Everything was suddenly about discovering God's plan for her life. Everything became a symbol—a sign."

"And now?"

"Now, she's leaving me surveys on life satisfaction. It's like she looks at me sometimes with pity and concern. It's like she thinks she needs to parent me—us." Norah's voice rose with excitement.

"Okay, honey, slow down."

Honey. How long since he'd called her that?

Tom cleared his throat in the sudden silence between them that indicated she had heard the term of endearment and been equally surprised. "But if we do the Christmas trip, we can work this out when we're all together."

"No. Don't you see? If I'm right, she would see that as our 'correcting the error of our ways,' but when nothing came of it she'd be even more disappointed than ever."

"So now what?"

"Well, so now—" Her voice faltered. "I don't know," she admitted. "What do you think?"

"I think we remember that we are dealing with a thirteen-year-old, and if you're determined not to come for Christmas, then Bella and I will go on to Hawaii as planned. What are you going to do for the holiday?"

This time the length of her silence was alarming. "Norah?"

She released a strangled little laugh. "I'll be fine. I thought I'd paint Izzy's room and update it—it's still a little girl's room and—"

"Isn't that something you want to do with her? Be sure she likes it?"

"Oh, she's dropped enough hints that I'm pretty sure I can pull it off. It'll be my Christmas present to her."

"You'll hire a decorator," Tom said. "Good

idea. How about I pitch in half? I never know what to give her."

"Oh, Tom, she's thirteen. Give her a shopping spree or a gift card or—"

"Because if we go in together on a gift you think she'll take it the wrong way?"

"Something like that," Norah admitted.

"Okay, you win that one. Now tell me what's going on with you?"

Again the laugh that came out was more of a bark. "I'm fine. Just fine."

"Don't tell me we're back to that."

"What?"

"Fine," Tom answered in falsetto.

Norah laughed and it was the laughter he knew so well—warm and rich, rising from somewhere deep inside her. "Get some sleep," she said. "And thanks."

"Good night, Norah."

"You're in a good mood," Izzy noted the following morning as she sat at the kitchen counter eating her breakfast.

"I am," Norah agreed as if she hadn't really noticed until Isabella mentioned it.

"How come?"

I talked to your father and—

Norah shrugged. "It's a beautiful day?"

"Yeah, like just about every other day in Phoenix," Izzy answered, her eyes narrowing. "Has something happened?"

"Does something have to happen for me to be happy? More to the point, does something have to happen to make you happy? And if so, what is it?"

"Whoa!" Isabella threw up her hands in a defensive pose. She scowled as she digested the sudden shift in the conversation's focus. "We were talking about you, remember?"

Norah waved a dismissive hand. "Enough about me. I'm boring. You, on the other hand, have a great many things going on—school, choir, the holiday concert at church…."

"I'm not doing that this year," Izzy mumbled around a mouthful of cereal.

"Why not?"

"Just decided I didn't want to do it."

"Are MJ and Ginny going to be in it?"

A shrug.

"Hey, what's going on?"

"Nothing. I've got to get my backpack. The bus'll be here."

Norah stepped around the edge of the kitchen island and stopped her flight. "Izzy, we need to talk. I know this isn't the right time, but tonight." It wasn't a question.

"Whatever," Izzy muttered and ran out the back door.

Norah watched her trudge down the driveway, shrugging into her backpack as she went. The bus arrived seconds later and Izzy disappeared inside. *Tonight,* she thought. *We're going to work this out. Please, God, help me find the words to make this better.*

As she mentally sent up the prayer, Norah realized that lately she had found renewed comfort and support in a faith she had put on the back burner for so many years. Izzy was right about one thing—Denver had changed her. Seeing Tom in person had allowed her to finally let go of her suppressed anger and bitterness over the divorce. She hoped he'd found similar forgiveness. Maybe it was possible for the two of them to truly share in Isabella's life instead of clinging to carefully laid out guidelines set forth in the divorce settlement.

Next year, she thought. *I'm just not ready to share Christmas—the memories are too precious, too close to my heart still. By next Christmas I'll be ready,* she promised.

Chapter Eight

For Tom weekend days were little different from weekdays. He got up, shaved, dressed, stopped at the local coffeehouse for his usual three-shot extra-hot espresso and headed for the office. On rare occasions he would work from home, telling himself he could use a day off. This was one of those days.

He sat on the terrace of his penthouse condominium and stared out at the Golden Gate Bridge and the sparkling waters of San Francisco Bay. Once—when Norah had been pregnant with Isabella—they'd taken a driving trip into the beautiful northern California countryside. Along the way they had stopped to marvel at the redwood forests and videotape each other striking silly poses comparing their height to the giant trees or mimicking a sea lion's crazy waddle. He wondered if Norah still had those tapes—and more important, did she ever watch them?

They hadn't had a lot of money in those days, so they had camped using a tent and sleeping bags borrowed from friends and cooking over an open fire. Norah had laughed and called this their pioneer period. At night when the temperatures dropped and the fog rolled in damp and chilling, they would snuggle together and plan their future.

A house of their own, kids—lots of kids. Maybe a dog—Norah wasn't so sure about bunches of kids *and* a dog. She had hinted that cats were less work.

"Than kids?" he had teased.

"Than kids and dogs," she had corrected. Then she had sighed and added, "But not half so much fun. Let's start with the kids."

And they had made love under the stars with the sound of the ocean and the crackle of a wood fire, the only background music they needed.

What happened, Norah?

The truth was that he couldn't get Norah's call off his mind. There had been something else—something beyond Isabella. He might have been out of her life for the last five years, but he knew this woman almost as well as he knew himself. They had practically grown up together. On their way to falling in love they'd been the best of friends, confiding and trusting in each other without question. Somewhere along the way in those married years, they'd lost some of that. And certainly during the time they'd been stranded together in Denver there had been times when she'd looked at him with that same distrust, that same questioning of his motives.

On the other hand there had also been times when he'd seen in her eyes the same desire he'd felt—the desire to turn back the clock.

Could they go back? At least to the point where they could once again have that friendship? Not just for the times when they needed to talk about their daughter, but also for the times when they needed a real friend. He could use a friend like Norah. And he had the feeling that there were times when Norah could as well.

"Like now," he muttered aloud. "What's going on with you now, Norah Jenkins Wallace, and why won't you let me help?"

His cell phone vibrated against the glass-topped table, startling him. He stared at it as if willing the caller to be Norah. He flipped open the cover. *Bella.*

"Hi, sweetie. What's up?"

"Daddy, have you talked to Mom lately? Like today?"

"Well no, is something wrong?"

"I don't know. The other day she had me go to

MJ's house after school—which is not all that unusual. She's as bad as you are sometimes when she gets to working on a project, but when she came to pick me up she was acting weird."

"Weird how?"

"Like overly cheerful, chattering on about the holidays and how much fun I was going to have with you if we changed plans and went to Wisconsin. She's all, 'Maybe there will be snow, but not until the planes have safely landed,' and stuff like that."

"Sounds pretty normal to me. You know how she's always been about the holidays."

"Yeah, but this was seriously over the top. And then we were supposed to have this big talk—which I had successfully avoided for days—and—"

Tom saw an opportunity to get Isabella to open up. "Talk about what?"

"Just stuff—that's not the important thing, Dad. The important thing is that all of a sudden she suggested we watch a movie together, so I agreed and she puts in this old-time one with Barbra Streisand and Robert Redford."

"The Way We Were," Tom said.

"Yeah, that one, and she starts sobbing about halfway through and doesn't stop. I mean we are talking close to hysterics here. It's a sad story, but it's just a dumb movie."

"It's always been her favorite movie," Tom reminded Isabella.

"Yeah, for times when she's feeling like the world's coming to an end or something," Bella replied. "She must have watched it eighty gazillion times after you guys split up."

"When did you get so smart?"

Bella gave a sigh of relief. "So you see the problem? I mean at first I thought this had to be about something I've done—or not done. Look at the chain of events—need to talk, but first the movie—maybe, so I feel really guilty—and then nothing."

"She's worried about you, sweetie," Tom admitted. "She tells me you've been pulling back from activities you once enjoyed."

"It's not that—well, it is that but not this. *We never talked.* It was like she'd forgotten all about that. I mean something has seriously happened, Dad."

"Have you asked her about it?"

"Dad!" Bella let out an exaggerated sigh of frustration. "Figure it out. One day she goes off to work all happy-happy, then she's practically a basket case. It's like she's waiting for something to happen. It's got to be her job."

"And you want me to do what?"

"Call her. I mean, who are the grown-ups here?"

"You know, Bella, in spite of what happened in Denver, not that much has changed between your mom and me."

"You guys were kissing, Dad."

So she'd seen that and then the following day with her hopes sky high, he and Norah had brought them crashing back to earth by going their separate ways as if nothing had changed.

"She was upset. Don't read anything into that."

"She's still upset and somehow I don't think my kissing her will have the same effect."

"Okay, I'll call her," Tom said. "But if she doesn't open up, Bella, we need to leave it alone."

"It's that boss of hers," Bella grumbled. "I never liked him."

"Luke? I thought the three of you had had some good times together."

"Please," Bella huffed. "He's a user and a loser."

"Your mom seemed to like him."

"Well, yeah, I guess if that's the only game in town."

Tom smiled to himself. "One day when you're older—"

Isabella groaned. "Dad, come into the twenty-first century. Mom went out with Luke because he was available and then he dumped her for Abby who I'll grant you is younger and has a better bod and—"

There's nothing wrong with your mother's body.

"Well, whatever your opinion may be, your mother has a right to a social life and that means she gets to choose the people she shares that life with. Just like I do. You don't get to dictate that, Bella."

"I'm not dictating anything. Is it so hard for you guys to understand that all I want is for both of you to be happy?" She paused. "Please tell me you are not still seeing Tabitha."

"Tamara. And where do you get the idea that your mother and I aren't—content with our lives?" Tom wanted to assure her that he was perfectly happy and he was pretty sure Norah was, but all of a sudden he saw that for the lie it would be—at least for him.

"Content? You're settling for *content?*"

"All right, I'll call your mother," he promised. "But I'm going to need some reason, so let's talk about you, young lady. Now what's all this nonsense about not being part of the youth choir concert?"

"She's fine," Tom assured Norah later that day. "We talked about the choir thing and she's promised to reconsider that. Seems she had decided it was a 'kid' thing."

"She's not fine, Tom," Norah argued. "And this is not about the youth choir. That was simply something I used to illustrate how she's changed since Thanksgiving."

"Okay, so give me another illustration."

"Last night we were watching a movie—"

"The Way We Were."

"Oh, she mentioned that. Well, did she also mention that when I got caught up in the story and started crying, she acted as if I were suddenly having a mental breakdown?"

Tom couldn't help it. He laughed. "That's not exactly her take on the situation."

"Really?" Norah's tone was suddenly overly polite and formal.

"Yeah, really. She's worried about you, Norah—and frankly so am I. What's going on at work?" He could tell that the sudden shift in topics had thrown her and knew that she was taking the time she needed to form her answer—an answer structured so as not to let him in.

"We're talking about Izzy," she said.

"Nice try. Answer the question. Something happened at work. Bella picked up on it and the other night when you and I were talking I thought there was more going on than just being worried about our daughter. So tell me."

"It's nothing I can't handle," she hedged.

Tom let the silence that followed that remark

stretch into several seconds. "Why do you do that, Norah? Shut people out?"

"I don't," she objected.

"You do. You started when we were married."

"You were the one always tied up in other things," she said softly. "There were times when I had to make decisions, had to handle things on my own."

"I was working." Tom felt the long-buried but all-too-familiar bile of his guilt at not having been there more and at the same time the certainty that he had been doing what was best for his wife and child.

This time it was Norah who allowed the silence to linger before she said, "Let's not do this."

"All I'm trying to say is that I'm here now, Norah." It was as close as he was capable of coming to a confession that maybe he could have made better use of his time in the years they were married. "Talk to me—as a friend."

When she didn't say anything right away, Tom pressed his case. "In spite of everything that's happened, Norah, we've always had that—we had that first. The kind of trust between best friends was our foundation."

"Yeah." Her voice was muffled but the single word was clear enough that he knew she'd started to cry.

"Ah, Norah, honey, don't. Just tell me. Maybe I can help."

"It is work," she admitted. "We didn't get the grant I was telling you about when we were in Denver."

"I'm sorry."

"Yeah, well, these things happen."

"But there's more than that—I mean this isn't the first time you've been turned down for a grant."

She sniffed and gave a shaky little laugh. "You're right. Why am I getting so worked up over one lost grant? Must be hormones or something."

Tom frowned. Never in all the years he'd known her had Norah ever blamed an emotional outburst on female physiology. In fact, she had little patience with women who did. She was gently but firmly shutting him out. And why not? It had been five years. Two days stranded in an airport could not erase that, so he decided to back off. "So what's Bella's last day of school before the holiday break?"

He heard her breathe a sigh of relief that he was letting it go and changing the subject. "Tuesday. I've made the airline reservation for Wednesday."

"We could still all go to Wisconsin together." *Why did he keep bringing that up?* She'd given her reasons and he really couldn't argue with them. But ever since he'd watched them get on that plane back to Phoenix, he'd been thinking about when they might see each other again.

"Oh, Tom, let it go."

"It's just an idea," Tom said. "You know, I've got to admit that Bella wasn't the only one who felt a little cheated when we never got that Thanksgiving back home together."

"I know. I felt that too. But trying to re-create that just won't work," Norah replied.

"We'll never know if Bella and I head off to Hawaii."

Her silence spoke volumes and he knew he should let it go. He searched his brain for something he could say that would keep her on the line.

"Well," she said, her voice steady once again. "Thanks for talking to Isabella and for—"

"She's just worried about you," Tom said. "Hey, Norah? Think about all of us getting together with the folks, okay? I can understand why not Christmas, but maybe springbreak or next summer?"

"Maybe," Norah agreed. "Bye, Tom."

When Norah put down the phone and turned around, Isabella was standing in the doorway. She realized that Izzy had been there for some time and that she'd heard at least her side of the conversation. She met her daughter's sullen glare.

"That was your father," she said unnecessarily.

"No, that was *your* opportunity," Isabella replied and turned for her dramatic exit.

"Isabella, sit down," Norah instructed.

Her daughter flung herself onto the sofa. Norah took the rocking chair across from her. "I am worried about you," she began. "You're setting yourself up to be hurt and I don't know how to stop that."

"You and Dad still love each other," Isabella said tightly.

"Yes, but it's not the kind of love you think. It's not romantic love."

Isabella snorted. "That kiss in the chapel sure looked romantic to me and I was half out of it."

Norah tried turning the tables. "You read that wrong, Izzy."

"Yeah, that's kind of what Dad said when I mentioned it to him."

"Okay," Norah said, slowly buying time as she considered how to navigate this detour in the conversation. "Your father and I kissed. But—"

Suddenly Isabella sat up straight and faced Norah directly. "No buts. Don't try to tell me it was just something that came about because you were worried about me and upset and Dad was just trying to comfort you. He could have hugged you or patted your hand to comfort you. He could have offered you his handkerchief to comfort you. *He kissed you.*"

And I kissed him back, Norah thought.

"And do *not* tell me it was a mistake."

"Why don't you tell me what you think," Norah said. "Why don't you tell me what you think all of this means—the getting stranded in Denver, the kiss, everything."

Izzy's eyes widened in surprise and disbelief. "You really want to know?"

"I do." Norah leaned back and started rocking as she fought to give every appearance that Izzy had her full and rapt attention.

"Well, after I sort of found out that Dad planned to be in Wisconsin—"

"Sort of?"

"Okay, I knew," she admitted. "So when we were headed there too, well, it was like sort of a sign."

"Why didn't you tell me that your dad was going?"

"Because I just knew you'd change your mind and decide not to go. I mean that's been the pattern, right? Every single time there's been the slightest chance the two of you might actually be in the same place at the same time, one of you found a way to jinx it."

"That's an exaggeration, but go on."

"So then we get to Denver and there's Dad big

as life, so sign number two." Isabella held up two fingers to emphasize the point. "*Then* He sends the storm." She raised a third finger and smiled triumphantly.

"He as in God?"

"Well, duh!"

Norah rocked forward and rested her elbows on her knees and her face in her hands before looking up at her daughter. "Izzy, I know your faith in God is very strong. It's also very new. Think about it. Why would God inconvenience thousands of people just so your father and I could be together? Especially when we were all going to be together in Wisconsin anyway? It doesn't make any sense."

"Mom, in Wisconsin you would have found ways to avoid him. In the airport there was no such chance *plus* God gave me just enough of an appendicitis flare-up so the two of you had to bond."

Norah opened her mouth to dissect that logic, but Isabella wasn't done.

"*And* it wasn't just about us. Other people were touched in a good way by that blizzard."

Norah couldn't come up with any argument for that. "Still—"

Isabella stood up, hands on hips. She seemed to tower over Norah. "No. You were almost there— back together but you pulled away. Well, thankfully

God is patient. So I will keep praying that there will be another chance for both of you, okay?"

"Okay." Norah smiled up at her beautiful daughter. "In the meantime—"

"In the meantime, you could seriously think about us all three going to Wisconsin and see what happens."

When Norah got to work on Monday she was fully prepared for a showdown with Luke. Instead she was surprised to see Stan Morrison, the agency's founder, in Luke's office. Luke was gesturing wildly, while Stan sat quietly in the single visitor's chair.

"What's up?" she asked Abby.

"Nobody knows. Dr. Morrison was here when Luke and I got here—separately," she added, blushing furiously. "Just at the same time."

"Abby, it's common knowledge that you and Luke are together. If he makes you happy, then there's nothing wrong with that."

"I just—I mean there was a time when you and Luke—"

"Ancient history," Norah assured her. "So did Stan say anything?"

"Not really. He was very pleasant like always and asked if he and Luke could talk in Luke's office."

"Well, whatever it is, I have work to do," Norah said as she headed for her cubicle. She was glad to see that the rest of the staff followed her lead. Only Abby lingered a moment before coming over to Norah's desk.

"Norah, did you call Dr. Morrison?"

"No. Why would I do that?"

Abby shrugged. "It's just that Luke had hinted that he might have to downsize the staff and that you were the person he was thinking of asking to accept a severance and—well, we all know you and the professor are good friends."

Norah raised her voice just enough so that everyone in the small office could hear her response. "It's true that after the news broke that we didn't get the grant, Luke tried to fire me. There was no mention of a severance package and my leaving was not a request. I suggested that he would need to make a valid case based on performance for letting me go. We left it at that and I assumed we would continue the discussion after the afternoon meeting."

"The meeting Luke cut out on and you conducted," said one of the male staff members who no longer pretended not to be listening.

"That's right. When Luke didn't come back, I left the ideas we'd developed on his desk."

Just at that moment the door to Luke's office

opened and Luke strode through the front office and out the back exit.

"Ladies and gentlemen, I wonder if you would all join me in the conference room," Dr. Morrison said in his usual calm, even tone.

Chapter Nine

"So Luke's gone?" Isabella said that night as she and Norah shared a supper of spaghetti, salad and garlic toast.

Norah nodded and slurped down a long strand of pasta.

"What did he do and how did the professor know?"

"Well, what I didn't know until today was that Carol Williams of the foundation had already called Stan when I talked to her. I thought her reasons for why we didn't get the funding were vague, but I never suspected this."

"This what?" Izzy said.

"It seems that Luke has a gambling problem himself. And a member of the foundation board had seen him in the casino."

"What was the board member doing there?"

"Well, sweetie, not everyone who enters a casino is a gambling addict. For some people it's just entertainment."

"So Luke could have just been out for some entertainment," Izzy reasoned.

"He could have, but the board member couldn't help noticing that everyone seemed to know him—the dealers, the waitresses and others. The board member asked some questions and learned that Luke was indeed a regular—and that he occasionally lost a great deal of money."

"I knew it," Isabella crowed. "I never liked him. So then what happened?"

"Oh, Izzy, this is a man's life, not some adventure show on television."

"I know." She pasted on a serious and concerned expression and concentrated on her dinner for a minute. Then she looked up, grinned and asked, "But what happened?"

"Carol told Stan that the foundation was willing to reconsider funding the program on one condition—that there be a full audit of the books and that Luke be replaced as head of the agency."

"Fired?"

"Demoted."

"But he's gone."

"He resigned."

"So who's going to head up the agency?"

"Stan will step in temporarily."

Norah cleared the dishes.

"You could do it," Izzy said quietly. "You've practically been doing it ever since Dr. Morrison left. Maybe you should go for it."

Norah stood very still, her hands filled with dirty dishes. "Do you know what you're suggesting?"

Izzy shrugged. "Hey, if God wants us all to be together something like a job is not going to stand in the way. You might as well be happy."

Thank you, Norah whispered, casting her eyes heavenward and then she put the dishes in the sink and hugged Izzy. "Have I told you recently what a terrific kid you are?"

Izzy pulled away, but she was grinning. "Better let me do the dishes while you go dig up the old résumé, Mom."

Norah went to the den and dug through a file drawer until she unearthed her résumé, badly in need of updating. After typing the information on the computer and staring at it for several minutes, she reached for the phone. But who would she call? If she called one of her coworkers or a peer at another nonprofit the word would be out that she was applying for the top post—or worse, that she was actively seeking another position. And for now all she was doing was taking a tentative first step just in case.

I could call Tom.

Norah dismissed the idea out of hand. Why Tom? What did he know of résumés?

He can look at it from the point of view of an employer.

True, but—

And he's not going to spread the word that you might be out there looking or going for the top job. No one will know and you'll still have the option of changing your mind.

Maybe. Norah played with the mouse, rolling the cursor over the screen, bringing up her e-mail. All spam.

Delete. Delete. I could probably find everything I need online, she reasoned.

Sure, but you'd still want somebody to look it over and besides you need to let Tom know that things seem to be back to normal with Izzy. After all, she's the one who encouraged you to go for the job. Hopefully that's a sign that she's finally accepted the way things are.

Before she could change her mind, Norah typed up a message entitled "Good News," attached her résumé—after working it over herself for half an hour, entered Tom's e-mail address and hit Send.

Tom understood that he should be glad that Norah was finally recognizing her own worth.

The fact was that the agency should have promoted her instead of hiring Luke, but she hadn't applied. And the news that applying for the top job had been Isabella's idea was good, right? So how come he felt this vague sense of disappointment? What was that about?

Maybe it was that she was moving forward with her life. *And I'm not?*

It was an unsettling idea. Tom had always believed that of the two of them, he was the one who had always had his eye on the future. In the early years the plans he'd made had been for the two of them and then after Isabella came along, he'd felt driven to secure a future for the three of them. But Norah had never shared that drive and they had argued often about his need to make sure that at least financially they had no worries.

"It's the one thing I can control," he'd told her.

"Why do you have to *control* anything?" she'd answered.

And now he couldn't help admitting that while she had looked for work that had meaning and purpose for her, regardless of the pay, early on he had gotten into the habit of considering every career move from the standpoint of what it would mean financially. He wanted the best for his family—the best schools for his children, the best opportunities for travel and—

Tom leaned back and looked around his spacious office. The walls were covered with tastefully framed awards and plaques recognizing his contributions to various organizations in the community. Every one of them represented a business opportunity rather than the kind of altruism they might have illustrated if it had been Norah's name on the certificate.

Beyond the solid Brazilian wood double doors stood a half dozen cubicles housing paralegals, administrative assistants and more staff to handle billing and research. Next door to either side of his office were the offices—almost as luxurious—of the attorneys he had taken on as partners. At the far end of a long hallway was the conference room, surrounded by frosted glass etched with the firm's logo. Everything was a distinct marker of the incredible prosperity he had achieved starting with the day his divorce from Norah had become final and he had bought out his share of the firm and gone into practice for himself. Stung by the finality of the divorce and the feeling of failure that came along with it, he had needed to excel at something. He would show her. And by the time his anger and hurt had subsided into a dull bruise rather than the open wound it had been, working sixteen-hour days had become a lifestyle.

As he reviewed Norah's employment history he saw his success for the hollow victory that it was. He glanced back at Norah's résumé still posted on his computer screen. He knew her to be a woman who had joined the agency because she truly believed she could make a difference for the people the agency served. He knew her as a woman of ideas, who believed anything was possible. None of that came through in the abbreviated sentences that described her responsibilities in each position she'd held. As usual she was underselling herself. Tom turned on the tracker tool and began striking her passive words and adding his own. And as he did he rediscovered that sense of excitement and energy he and Norah had once shared as teenagers and then young adults when everything seemed possible. *When the two of them had dreamed of making a real difference—of changing the world.*

"Wow!" Norah said the next day when she called to thank him. "Who is this woman?"

She's the girl who blew me away when we were the boy and girl next door back in Normal, Wisconsin. She's the one who showed me that even kids from small farm towns can set the world on fire. She's the woman who stole my heart and gave me a daughter who gives purpose to my life.

"It's all true and you know it. If anything, I've understated some of it."

"I doubt it," Norah said and he could hear in her voice how pleased and flattered she was.

"Are you accusing me of bias?"

"Not at all. I am on my knees thanking you," she said laughing. "If I decide to submit this the search committee is going to be superimpressed."

"What do you mean 'if'?"

"It's just that Stan seems to be enjoying being back. He never was very high on the idea of retirement and—"

"So you think he might stay on?"

"The board is accepting résumés, but nothing's going to happen until after the holidays. I just don't want to be in competition with Stan."

"Does he know you're interested?" Tom felt a tug of irritation at Norah's mentor. This was her time, her chance. Stan had had his.

"We really haven't discussed it. Speaking of job changes, did Izzy tell you her friend MJ's dad is being transferred. They'll be moving the first of the year."

"How's she taking that?"

"Pretty well. The transfer is to Minneapolis, so she and MJ are already making plans to get together whenever Izzy comes to Wisconsin. I heard the two of them talking about some music camp in Wisconsin the other night. If I go for the job and get it, then maybe—"

Tom frowned. "If you think music camp is right for Bella, then she should go to music camp. We have the money for whatever Isabella needs, whether you decide to take the job or not, Norah."

"I know," she said softly. "I didn't mean to sound like—I was just thinking out loud."

"Norah? This going for the job? It isn't about whether you'd be doing the best thing for Bella or competing with Stan. Do it—or don't—for only one reason."

"Because it's best for me?" she said.

"That's my girl," he replied. "I've got an appointment. Tell Bella I'll call her later to finalize travel plans."

On the Wednesday before Christmas Norah drove Izzy to the airport. As further proof of her acceptance of the way things were, Isabella had made the final decision about the trip—she and Tom would travel to Hawaii as planned.

"But you promise to seriously think about us all meeting at the grands over springbreak?" Izzy asked on the drive to the airport.

"I promise to seriously think about it," Norah replied. "You didn't gift wrap anything that you're carrying on, did you?" Norah focused on navigating the multiple lanes of the highway.

"Mother, this is not exactly my first flight. I do know the rules."

"Just checking." She switched lanes, waving to the driver who had opened a spot for her. They rode in silence, but Norah was glad to realize that it was not the strained silence of the last few weeks. This time it was comfortable—each of them gathering their thoughts as they looked ahead to the busy day before them.

"Are you going to submit your résumé today?" Izzy asked.

"Probably," Norah hedged. "We'll see."

"Mom! Today's the deadline. Do you want to end up working for another Luke?" She shuddered. "Yuck!"

Norah laughed. It was so good to have things back on track with her daughter.

As Norah parked in short-term near the departure terminal, Izzy was checking her phone for messages, then the weather. "Snowing in Wisconsin," she announced. "Eighty and sunny in Hawaii." She leaped from the car and started pulling her luggage from the trunk. A skycap hovered nearby.

"I've got it, thank you," Izzy said politely as she rummaged through the pockets of her jeans until she came up with two single dollar bills. She handed them to the skycap and grinned. "But Merry Christmas!"

Norah could hardly wait to tell Tom what their daughter had done unprompted. When they reached security, she hugged Izzy hard. "Have a wonderful time and don't worry about anything back here," she instructed. "I'll call you," she shouted as Izzy disappeared down the concourse.

When she reached her office the message light on her phone was blinking madly. Norah dropped her purse on the desk along with the flat briefcase that contained—among other files—her résumé and application for the director's position. She sat down and picked up the receiver, punching in the code for retrieving her messages.

"You have two messages. Message one sent at seven-twenty this morning."

Norah frowned and pulled a notepad closer, prepared for the emergency a call at that early hour might indicate.

"Hi," Tom said, his voice a little thick from sleep and no coffee. "Just wanted to wish you luck with the job thing. I know you won't hear until after the New Year, but this is a big first step, Norah. Just remember, you deserve this and you *are* hands down the best candidate for this job no matter who else applies. I'll call later so you know Bella arrived safely."

Norah's finger hovered over the number that would delete the message and move her forward to message number two. But then she slid her finger to a different key—the one that would save the message so she could listen to it again—listen to Tom believing in her again—and again.

"Message two sent at seven-sixteen this morning."

At first there was silence, although Norah could hear voices in the background, muffled but urgent sounding as if the caller had a hand over the receiver. She turned up the volume and strained to hear. She pulled the notepad closer.

"Norah, this is Eleanor."

Tom's mother. Why was her ex-mother-in-law calling her?

"I called you at home but you and Isabella must have already left for the airport and I don't have the number for her cell."

What's happened? Norah felt her heart skip a beat, then lurch into race mode.

"I'm here with your parents. Earle collapsed while shoveling snow this morning. The paramedics are taking him to the hospital now—possible heart attack. Irene is here with him and I'll follow the ambulance with her. He's conscious and—we're going now, dear. The number at the hospital is—"

Norah waited, pen poised as Eleanor repeated the number someone in the background dictated.

"Everything will be fine," Eleanor assured her. "We'll call as soon as we know anything more."

The recorded voice repeated instructions to follow to delete or save the message—twice. Finally Norah simply hung up the phone.

"Norah?"

Stan Morrison was standing at the entrance to her cubicle. She looked up at the man's kind, weathered face and burst into tears. At the same time, her phone started to ring.

"Somebody get that," Stan instructed as he knelt beside Norah's chair, one hand hovering uncertainly around her shoulders. "What's happened?"

Norah started to tell him, the words coming in between gulps of tears.

"It's your husband," Abby said quietly indicating Norah's phone.

Stan lifted the receiver and handed it to Norah while everyone on the staff gathered around, uncertain of what they should do, but prepared to do anything they could.

"Norah? Mom just called. I'm on my way to the airport to meet Bella, but I've got my assistant working to put everything in place to get you there as soon as possible. Now listen to me." He began rattling off a long list of instructions. *Go home...pack...sending driver...airport....*

"Tom?" Norah said, stopping him. "Bella's going to be so upset. Will you come with her?"

"Oh, honey, where else would I go?"

Chapter Ten

At the airport check-in, Norah was informed that she had been upgraded to first class. *Tom,* she thought. Just before boarding her flight, Norah was finally able to reach the hospital and her mother.

"Yes, it was a heart attack—mild, according to the doctor. A warning, he called it."

"How's Dad doing?"

Her mother sighed. "You know your father. He didn't finish shoveling the front walk and now he's concerned that it will ice over and someone will fall. Eleanor said she would see to it, but now Dad's all worried that she'll ask Dan to shovel and *he'll* end up in the hospital as well."

"Tom and Izzy can take care of it when they get there," Norah said.

There was a beat and then her mother said. "You're all coming? Together?"

It was impossible not to understand the note of hope in those questions.

"We're all on our way," Norah assured her. "Izzy left for California this morning. She and Tom will fly out from there today or tomorrow. I should be there late this afternoon."

"I'll tell your father. That should perk him up."

"Mom? He's going to be okay, right?"

"He'll be fine," her mother assured her, but her tone was too bright, too upbeat. "You just worry about yourself. We'll see you when you get here."

She tried Tom's phone and Izzy's, but got voice mail in both cases. *They must be on their way.* The thought gave her enormous comfort as she settled back in the wide seat and closed her eyes, hardly aware that the plane had started to taxi down the runway.

This trip the flight was smooth and mere background noise for the emotional turbulence Norah was feeling. Anxiety was uppermost—the fear that her father's condition was far more serious than her mother was willing to admit. The sudden panic that she might not make it back to Wisconsin in time to tell him how much she loved him, how much he had meant to her. The uncertainty of what his health might mean for the future.

Then there was work. Stan had suggested she

take the remainder of the year off. "Come back fresh after the New Year," he'd said as he walked her out to her car.

Norah thought about the file folder containing her application that was still lying on her desk. All she needed to do was call Stan or Abby and let them know the folder was there. But she didn't. What if her father died? What if he was permanently incapacitated? How would he and Mom manage in a house where all the bedrooms and the single bath were upstairs? As an only child she felt enormous responsibility for the well-being of her parents—she just hadn't thought the need would come so soon.

Underlying everything was an almost suffocating sense of guilt. Guilt that she had chosen to live so far away that her parents rarely had the opportunity to spend time with her or Izzy—their only grandchild. Guilt that there weren't more grandchildren. Guilt that her marriage had failed and that the combination of the end of her marriage and the fact that she and Tom had not had more children and that she had willingly—blithely—continued to reside halfway across the country—for what? Warm weather?

Her parents had never been anything but thrilled for her happiness and concerned for her heartaches. Even though she realized that in the rubble of her own dreams for the future lay their dreams for her and for their own golden years when their friends were intricately involved in the lives of their adult children and grandchildren.

You can always come home.

From the time Norah had been a small child and all through college and her adult years, that had been her mother's message to her. Never said in a whining wishful tone, but rather offered as a haven—an assurance that whatever happened in her life there was this one place where she would be loved unconditionally.

"Ms. Wallace?"

Norah blinked up at the flight attendant.

"I have a message for you." He handed her a folded piece of paper. "I—is there anything I can get for you?"

The young man's expression was sympathetic.

"No, thank you," Norah whispered as she fingered the note, her heart in her throat. Judging by the steward's expression and the unusual delivery of a message in flight, her father must have taken a turn for the worse, but Mom would never handle things this way. Mom wouldn't begin to know how to contact her in midair. She opened the note and read the contents twice, then looked up at the steward.

"I don't understand," she said, handing him the note.

The young man took the empty seat next to her. "Arrangements have been made for you to take a private charter from O'Hare to Madison, Wisconsin," he read, then looked over at her. "I understand you are traveling for a family emergency?"

Norah nodded.

"Apparently someone has arranged to make sure you get there as soon as possible. We're approaching Chicago now. As soon as we land a skycap will be waiting with a cart to take you to the private flight." He stood up and handed her back the note. "I hope everything works out."

"Thank you," Norah murmured.

They landed twenty minutes later, but it took another twenty to reach the gate. Norah was first off the plane once the cabin door opened.

"Ms. Wallace?"

"Yes." Her voice shook and her legs suddenly felt like rubber.

"Hop in," the heavyset woman driver invited, and practically before Norah's feet cleared the floor, they were off. The driver wove in and out of throngs of travelers, beeping her horn and calling out cheerfully, "Stand back. Woman driver on the loose," to the delight and surprise of bored or harried passengers she passed along the way.

"Hang on, sweetie," she said as she made a sharp turn down a narrow passageway, threaded her way through what looked like a warehouse of baggage and out onto the tarmac. "Shortcut," she yelled over the sudden whipping wind. "You warm enough?"

Norah nodded and hung on to the front panel of the golf cart.

"Those your folks there?" The driver nodded toward a small private jet where miraculously Izzy and Tom were waiting—Izzy waving her arms as if directing the cart into a landing.

"Yes," Norah yelled back, her heart suddenly lighter. "Those are my folks."

"Wow, you landed yourself a major hottie, didn't you, girl?" The woman said as she whipped the cart to a halt and eyed Tom's approach.

Norah couldn't help it. She smiled even as tears glistened on her lashes.

"Ah, sweetie, it's all going to be okay," the woman assured her and Norah suddenly realized that the woman's act had been for her benefit to take her mind off whatever trouble she was flying in to face.

"Thank you," she said softly and squeezed the driver's gloved hand.

"This it?" Tom asked as he ran over to the cart and took her small duffel from her. He handed the driver a generous tip.

"Good looking and a good tipper," the woman said to Norah. "This one's a keeper," she advised as she waved and drove off.

Tom wrapped one arm around Norah's shoulders as if protecting her from the elements as he guided her toward the plane. "Get on board, Bella," he called.

As soon as Norah boarded, Isabella burst into tears.

"Oh, Izzy, it's going to be okay. I talked to Grandma and Papa's going to be okay. She says seeing you will be the best possible medicine."

Gently she fastened Izzy's seat belt and then her own as Tom gave final instructions to the pilot and then settled into the seat across from them. As the plane's twin engines revved and the pilot began the slow taxi toward the runway, Tom reached across the narrow aisle and took Norah's hand.

As soon as they landed in Madison, Tom led Norah and Isabella to the car he'd hired. It was waiting on the tarmac and Norah was grateful for Tom's thoughtfulness in getting them to the hospital as quickly as possible. This time instead of riding up front with the driver as he had in Denver when Bella was sick, he got into the backseat. He stretched one arm along the back of the seat so that Bella could rest her head against his shoulder and he could gently stroke Norah's hair with his fingers.

"What if Papa dies?" Bella murmured.

"Papa is not going to die—not yet," Tom said, but until they knew the full seriousness of Earle's condition, he was unwilling to make promises.

He glanced over at Norah. She was staring out the window, but he suspected she was not seeing any of the passing scenery as the driver headed for the medical complex on the campus of the University of Wisconsin. "They're the best, Norah," he said softly. "They've got the best specialists—the best trauma teams. He's in good hands."

Norah nodded but did not look away from the window. She was dry-eyed now, her face looking as if she had aged several years over the hours since she'd received the news. Tom was pretty sure that he knew what she was thinking, for they had often discussed how fortunate they were—and Bella was—that both sets of parents were in good health. Lively seniors who added a generational depth to Bella's life that she might have missed by not having siblings.

The driver turned onto the drive to the hospital entrance.

"Norah?" Tom said quietly and this time she

turned to look at him. But her eyes were devoid of anything more than exhaustion. "I'm sorry," he said and understood that under the circumstances she would take the words as comfort for her father's illness. Some day he would find a way to tell her that he was taking steps toward realizing what his pride had contributed to the downfall of their marriage.

A single tear coursed its way down Norah's left cheek. Tom reached over and wiped it away with his thumb.

The receptionist directed them to the cardiac intensive care unit waiting room. Norah hurried down the hall barely aware that Isabella was following reluctantly and that Tom had also held back to reassure their daughter. In this moment Norah was a daughter—an only child—who needed her own mother to calm her fears.

Tom's mother, Eleanor, was the only person in the waiting room other than a volunteer sitting at the desk and reading the newspaper. The minute Norah entered the room Eleanor was on her feet, coming forward, her arms outstretched. Norah did not hesitate to step into the circle of that embrace.

"Where's Mom?" she asked.

"She's in with Earle. The doctor's there now and—"

"I want to hear what he has to say," Norah said, breaking free and heading for the double doors that separated the patient unit from the waiting room. The volunteer made a move as if to stop her, but Eleanor interceded. "This is Mr. Jenkins's daughter," she explained even as she touched the large button on the wall that sent the double doors flying open with a whoosh. "Second room on the left," she told Norah.

Several nurses and a couple of doctors glanced up at the sound of the doors opening, but all but one returned to work. "May I help you?" the woman in a green smock asked.

"My father," Norah said and nodded toward the second sliding-glass door on the left where the curtains were pulled closed. "I—"

"Ah, you must be Norah," the woman replied. "Your parents have been expecting you. Doctor is in with them now—he just arrived, so you haven't missed much." She nodded toward the partially open door.

"Thank you," Norah said.

The news was good.

"You've dodged a bullet this time, young man," the doctor, who looked to be no more than thirty years old, said as he studied the chart and did not look at either of Norah's parents.

Norah saw her father frown and knew exactly

what was coming. First he glanced around the room as if trying to figure out who the doctor meant. Then his eyes widened and he pointed to himself. "Are you talking to me?" It was his best De Niro impression and Norah felt a smile tug at the corners of her mouth.

The doctor looked up, startled.

"Because my name is either Earle or Mr. Jenkins—take your pick. If we ever become really good friends I might even let you call me 'Early,' but that's unlikely. I am seventy-two years old—not young—old. Do we understand each other, *young man?*"

"Yes, sir," the doctor replied, all bravado gone.

"So, I've dodged a bullet," Earle prompted. "Define 'dodge.'"

The doctor put down the chart and moved closer to the bed. He positioned himself so that he included Norah and her mother in the conversation. In clear lay terms, he gave them a detailed diagnosis and then discussed changes and additions to Earle's diet and medications. He suggested that Norah's parents start walking daily or if that was impossible because of weather, then get a treadmill or exercise bike.

"We have one of each," Norah's mother told him. "In the basement."

"They make dandy clothes lines," Earle joked.

The doctor smiled—a real smile and Norah could not help noticing that he was giving no indication that he needed to get this over with and move on to other patients. "You'll be moved to our cardiac care unit this afternoon," he said. "We'll leave the monitor in place, so don't go trying any marathons, okay? But walks up and down the halls every few hours would be good. We'll see how you do for the next twenty-four hours and then talk about getting you out of here."

Norah's father offered the man a handshake. "Thanks, doc. Really. Thanks for everything."

The doctor returned the handshake and laughed. "You aren't getting rid of me that easily, sir. I'll be around this evening to check on you, okay?"

He nodded to both Norah and her mother and left the room. Norah could hear him repeating his orders to the nurse outside.

The minute the doctor was gone her father stretched out his arms to her. His eyes were misty but his embrace was strong. "How's my girl?" he said.

"Better now that I'm here," Norah admitted.

"Isabella off to Hawaii?" Earle asked.

"She's out in the waiting room—with Tom." Norah did not miss the look that passed between her parents—a look she well knew was filled with hope that this was a positive sign.

"Izzy had already left for California when Eleanor called Norah," Irene explained.

"Then Tom called," Norah added, "and—well, you know Tom. He practically hired Air Force One to get us here." Her voice trailed off as she realized she'd delivered this last not with her usual irritation at Tom's ability to buy whatever he needed, but rather appreciation for the fact that he was able to get her here in such good time.

"Do I get to see them or is Doctor Young Man still restricting my visitors?"

"You know the rules, Earle," Norah's mother said. "Only two visitors at a time—at least in this unit. Norah and I will step out so Izzy and Tom can come see you."

"Afraid that'll have to wait," the nurse announced. "Mr. Jenkins is going for some tests and then on to his new digs. You and the rest of the family can meet him up on the fourth floor in room—" She consulted a chart and gave them the room number all the while moving them out the door to make room for the orderlies who had come to transfer Earle.

In the waiting room they filled Eleanor in on the good news. "Where's Isabella?" Norah's mom asked, glancing around.

"She and Tom took a little walk," Eleanor said, glancing at Norah. "Isabella became quite upset. She was crying and Tom was having trouble consoling her. I think he was taking her in the direction of the coffee shop."

Norah looked at her mother. "You should get something to eat as well."

"Don't worry about me. Eleanor and I will get something. You go find Izzy and meet us in Dad's new room."

Tom and Izzy weren't in the coffee shop near the lobby. Nor were they in the cafeteria on the lower level. Spotting the volunteer she had seen in the waiting room, Norah stopped him and asked if he'd seen her daughter.

"You might try the chapel," he suggested. "It's just down the hall from the waiting room. Your little girl was pretty upset and that's a good quiet place to go."

"Thank you." Norah eased open the door to the chapel and heard Tom's low voice. He and Izzy were seated in the front row of chairs. Izzy had her face buried in her hands and was shaking her head vehemently from side to side as Tom tried to reason with her.

"Hey," Norah said as she slid into the seat on the other side of her and looked at Tom for answers. "What's going on?"

"Oh, Mom," Izzy wailed, throwing herself into Norah's arms. "It's all my fault—Papa's heart attack. It's my fault."

"Shh," Norah soothed.

"I tried to convince her," Tom said, his expression helpless and forlorn at his inability to handle this crisis. "I pointed out that she was miles away and had nothing at all to do with—"

This set off a fresh outburst of tears and Norah—relieved by the news that her father would be all right—suppressed a smile. "She's thirteen," she murmured to Tom. "Reason and logic are not yet part of her repertoire."

"I prayed," Izzy gulped out the words. "I prayed that God would do something that would get us all back together at least for the holidays. I prayed so hard—constantly."

"And you think God made Papa have a heart attack just so we would all be together?"

Isabella nodded and burrowed deeper into Norah's embrace. Tom looked as if he had just heard news beyond comprehension. "But, honey—" he said to Isabella as he rubbed her back.

Norah warned him with a look then started to speak quietly to Isabella. "Well, here's what I came to tell you. Papa is going to be just fine. The doctor is letting him move to a regular room as we speak and then if everything goes okay with the new medicine the doctor is giving him, he'll be able to go home maybe as soon as day after tomorrow."

Izzy grew still and her sobs dwindled to the occasional shuddering intake of breath. She sat up and looked at Norah. "Really?"

"Really. So you see, darling, everything is going to be all right. Your Papa will be home in a few days and we can help Grandma start getting everything set up for Christmas and—"

"We're staying for Christmas?" Izzy asked, looking from Norah to Tom and back again. "All of us?"

"And New Year's," Tom said, then he glanced at Norah. "If that's okay."

"Works for me," Norah said, ignoring the sudden increase in the rhythm of her heartbeat. After all, Tom would say anything right now to calm his daughter. "Of course, I wasn't on my way to Hawaii and the beaches full of cute boys."

Isabella smiled. "There are a couple of cute boys here," she said. "I met them last time I visited—at the church picnic, remember?"

At the church picnic, Norah thought. *Where Tom and I met when I was Izzy's age.*

"Can I see Papa now?"

"In a little while, once he gets back from some tests and settled in his new room. But both your grandmothers are in the coffee shop having lunch and I'm sure they would love to have you join them."

"*Us* join them," Isabella corrected. She stood up and faced the small altar. "You know what I was thinking?"

Tom stood behind her and placed his hands on her shoulders. "I'm almost afraid to ask."

"Daddy! This is serious."

"Okay, what?"

"I was thinking that this is the second time we've all ended up in some strange chapel—not our own church, but just this little place set aside for people in pain to work things out."

"God is everywhere," Norah said softly as she stepped to Izzy's side and took her hand.

"Exactly," Isabella replied, turning to gaze up at her parents. "Can we have a moment of silent prayer to thank God for taking care of Papa?"

"Sure, sweetie," Tom said.

"And feel free to thank Him for other stuff— you know, like us all being together for the holidays," Isabella suggested before bowing her own head.

Norah could not meet Tom's gaze over Izzy's bowed head, so she lowered her eyes and prayed.

Thank You, God, for caring for Dad. I know there will come a day when he and Mom won't be here, but not today—not this time. And, God, thank You for bringing Tom and me together again, but I am so worried that Isabella is going to be hurt. Please help her to see that being together as a family for the holidays is not the same as being back together. Please help her find ways to accept that and for us to move forward.

"Amen," Isabella said aloud, then grinned up at her parents. "Let's eat. I'm starved."

Norah's dad was an instant hit with the staff on the fourth floor. His room quickly became a gathering place for relieved friends and neighbors and Tom found himself observing the scene from a spot near the door. He watched Irene fuss over Earle and Earle lap up the attention at the same time he was chastising her to, "Stop hovering. That's what they pay those folks in uniform to do."

He saw the easy camaraderie between his parents and Norah's—the kind of intimacy that comes with having shared so many of life's adventures—first home, raising children, career triumphs and woes, traveling together and more. Two indestructible marriages made all the stronger because of the friendship between the couples.

His dad was relating a fishing story—one where Earle was the hero, having banished a snake sleeping under one of the seats of the boat once the friends had left shore and had nowhere to run. Tom watched his mother's face, knowing she must have heard this story a hundred times. But her expression showed no irritation at the repetition. Instead she was finishing his sentences, laughing with him. Tom guessed that she was admiring his father's determination to remind them all of other times, better times—times that they could all hope would come again and produce new stories to tell.

He watched Irene and Earle and his parents for several minutes. This was the model he and Norah had grown up with. This was what they had believed they would have. This was what had seemed to come so easily to their parents—and so hard for them.

He glanced over at Norah. She was laughing at the story, finding comfort in it. Some of the tension had gone out of her face and shoulders. She had one hand on the raised head of her father's bed. From time to time her eyes would flick over to the monitor, checking the graph and numbers there, reassuring herself that he was past the crisis. The way the afternoon sun fell across her cheekbones made her look young and vulnerable and he wanted more than anything to go to her, wrap his arms around her and assure her that it would all be okay.

Norah looked up then and her eyes met his. She seemed surprised to find him watching her and ducked her head in that shy girlish way that had always been her trademark. They had loved each other so deeply—like younger versions of their parents.

It wasn't the first time he'd thought about how it might be if they were to get back together. Ever since he'd seen them in Denver his thoughts had repeatedly drifted toward that fantasy. For surely that's all it was—all it could ever be after all this time.

Tom shook himself back to reality. The reality was that he had a law practice—one that employed several other people. Norah had her work—work that she was determined could make a real difference for others. She lived in Arizona. He lived in California. Normal, Wisconsin, was the past and no longer home for either of them. Ever pragmatic, Tom reminded himself that he was seeing everything through tinted glasses— lenses that filtered in the magic of the holidays plus the timely reminder that their parents—and they—were not getting any younger and clocks were ticking for all of them.

He looked down and saw that Norah had moved next to him. "Should we go back?" Norah was asking and at first Tom thought she might have read his mind. She had once been able to do that.

"Back?" *Could they? Was that even advisable?*

"To the house. Drop off our luggage and pick up some things that Mom needs?" She studied him and frowned. "Are you feeling all right, Tom?"

"Yeah. Sure." He moved a step away to avoid her hand raised to check his temperature as if he were Isabella. "Dad? Can we use the car?"

Both sets of parents burst out laughing.

"Have her home by ten," Earle instructed sternly, setting off yet another round of laughter among the four friends.

"I don't get it," Isabella said, then the light dawned. "Oh, like when they were dating?"

Norah gathered her jacket and purse. She looked up at Tom. "Ready?"

"It's a date," he replied, grinning mischievously.

"Cute."

Chapter Eleven

Norah's father came home two days later to a sidewalk and driveway completely clear of ice and snow and strict instructions from his doctor that shoveling—especially by hand—was no longer to be part of his chore assignment.

"What'd you do, Renie? Hire one of those plow services?" he asked his wife when he saw the driveway.

"Two nice young boys from the church youth group did the work and they charged a cup of hot cocoa and some of my peanut butter cookies," Norah's mom replied.

Earle had no response to that and slowly headed up the front walk to the house. But Irene was not finished with the topic. "Of course, there's still the issue of who will do the work going forward. Winter has just begun, you know."

"I know. I know," Earle grumbled.

"Well, no need to think about that right now," Tom said as he held the door open for Earle. "At least through the holidays you've got Isabella and me to handle that kind of thing."

Isabella made a face. "Dad!"

"Hey, it'll build character—not to mention muscles," Tom said and Earle chuckled for the first time since leaving the hospital. Norah could have hugged Tom and saw from her mother's expression that she wasn't the only one.

The phone was ringing when they got inside. "I'll get that," Irene said.

"Come on, Izzy," Norah said. "Let's start some lunch."

"Guess you get stuck talking to the invalid," Earle joked, looking up at Tom as he patted the chair next to him.

"We could play a game of chess," Tom suggested. "I'm a little rusty, but I think I still remember the moves." He took the chair opposite Tom's recliner. The chessboard was set for play on the coffee table between them.

From the kitchen hallway Norah watched her father ease himself into his chair, noting for the tenth time how his movements had become tentative and uncertain overnight. Tom caught her eye and she drew strength from his gaze—one that seemed to say, "It's all going to be okay."

"Thank you," she mouthed.

He smiled and turned his attention back to the chess game. "My first move, right?" he said as he slid a piece forward.

"Whoa!" Earle cried with delight. "You sure you want to start there?" And the game was on.

Over lunch, Irene reported that Eleanor had called to say that the women of the church had organized meals for the family for the coming week. "To give us time to catch our breath, according to Eleanor." Irene shook her head. "People can be so amazingly thoughtful."

The talk turned to preparations for the fast-approaching holiday.

"Fortunately I took care of my shopping before this little episode with my ticker," Earle reported with a wink. "But I could use some help with the wrapping." He turned to Norah and Isabella. "How are you girls at gift wrapping?"

"I'm kind of better at *un*wrapping," Isabella teased.

"We'll teach you," Norah and her father said at the same time and everyone laughed.

"We have to get a tree," Izzy said.

"Oh, darling, we should probably use the artificial tree this year, don't you think?" Irene asked.

"No," Norah said before Izzy could reply. "Let's have a real old-fashioned Christmas. You just leave everything to us."

"And Dad," Izzy added.

"At your service," Tom said with a mock salute to his daughter. He stood up. "Speaking of holiday preparations, I promised Mom I'd haul down the decorations from the attic. Thanks for lunch—and the chess game."

Under protest, Earle agreed to take a nap, while Norah and her mother cleared the lunch dishes and Isabella went upstairs to unpack and settle into her side of Norah's childhood room. Norah found her there, sitting against the headboard of one of the twin beds, writing in her journal.

Norah knew better than to ask what Izzy was writing. The journal had been part of her assignments as she prepared to join the church. Its contents were for Izzy's eyes only—and God's, of course. For the entries—at least early on—they were to be written in the form of letters to God. That had been the minister's idea as he sought a way to bring the reality of faith into each teen's life.

"Sometimes the concept of prayer can be intimidating to a teen," he had explained to the parents. "A journal seems more in touch with their need to communicate with God." He'd laughed then and added, "If I could come up with a way they could text God via cell phone, I'd use that."

Norah unpacked the few clothes she'd grabbed before heading to the airport. As she pushed back the sliding mirrored doors of the closet, she saw several items of clothing that she had left behind when she and Tom were married. But this time she found that she wanted the memories those clothes might evoke—memories of her youth, of living here with her parents. She pulled out a madras plaid shirt, a pair of cuffed jeans—the wide leather belt still threaded through the loops. Next to that was the silver jersey wrap dress she'd worn the night Tom proposed.

"What's all that stuff?" Izzy asked, putting her journal aside and scrambling to the foot of the bed to watch Norah.

"Memories," Norah said as she burrowed into the far corner of the closet and brought out a double-breasted navy wool coat with fur trim at the cuffs and collar. She slid it off the wooden hangar and tried it on, belting the waist with the wool sash. "What do you think?" she asked as she pirouetted in front of the mirror on the open closet door.

"I think it's got fur trim," Izzy said and made a face. "You wore that?"

"It was my Sunday coat when I was in college."

Norah reached onto the closet shelf and pulled down a hatbox. "Wait," she said and then squealed with delight as she pulled out a hat that matched the fur trim on the coat. She put it on and it slid down over her eyebrows. "I had long thick hair in those days," she explained.

"The coat's not terrible," Izzy announced as she surveyed the costume. "But that fur has to go. This is the twenty-first century, Mom. Hopefully we are slightly more enlightened?"

"Okay," Norah said as she replaced the hat in the box and took off the coat. "We'll remove the trim." She took a pair of scissors from a dresser drawer and started snipping threads. "Ta da!"

"Pretty cool," Izzy admitted. "Can I try it?"

"Sure."

They spent the rest of the afternoon trying on Norah's old clothes and rummaging through drawers to see what else Norah's mother had preserved. And there in the far back corner of a dresser drawer stuffed with old photo albums, yearbooks and long-forgotten term papers, Izzy found the prize.

"Ah ha!" she shouted triumphantly as she held aloft a small, green, leather-bound book with a gold-plated closure that locked and a tiny key dangling from a chain like a bookmark. "Your diary!" She hugged it to her chest.

"Hand it over," Norah said, grabbing for it and laughing.

"Do you think Grandma read it?" Izzy asked, dancing out of Norah's reach. "How could you leave your diary here?"

"I forgot it—didn't need it anymore." *Tom and I were married and that was all that mattered to me when I moved out of this room.* "Now give it up."

"Are you going to read it before you burn it?"

"Who says I'm going to burn it?"

"Must be some juicy stuff in here." Izzy mused. "I'll bet Dad would just love to know—"

"That's it." Norah dived for the book and they both ended up in a pile on the bed, laughing and gasping for air.

"Everything okay up there?" Earle shouted from the living room.

"Fine," Izzy and Norah shouted back in unison and then collapsed in a fresh fit of giggles.

"Well, some of the women from the church are coming up the front walk—looks like they're bringing enough to feed the neighborhood. You girls should come down and say hello," Irene called.

"Yes, ma'am," Norah and Izzy chorused.

"You girls?" Izzy whispered and fell back onto the bed laughing.

Norah took advantage of her daughter's distraction to grab Izzy's journal. "Trade you," she said.

"No fair," Izzy wailed, but she was still grinning as she handed over the diary that Norah took and stored inside the fur hat in the hatbox. "I know I can trust you but just to be sure," she said as she tied the ribbons of the hatbox into an intricate bow. "Now brush your hair and let's go make nice with the church ladies."

They had just finished supper when there was a light tap at the back door, and Isabella—now completely at home in her grandparents' house—ran to see who was there. "Dad!"

Then, as Tom entered the laundry room and wiped his feet, Izzy added, "Hey, it's snowing again."

Tom was wearing a black ski jacket that Norah remembered from their years of living in Normal along with a ridiculous pink and purple striped stocking cap. In his gloved hands he held three pairs of ice skates—one black men's pair and two pairs in the pristine white usually preferred by woman.

"Oh no, you don't," Norah said as soon as she saw the skates. "It's December. Is the ice on the pond even solid enough for skating?"

Tom grinned. "They've set up a new skating rink."

"That's right, Norah," her father said. "Just like

the professionals. It's downtown in the square—they can freeze it in the winter and then in the summer use it for concerts. It's pretty slick." He grinned at his own joke.

Izzy groaned and then laughed. "You are so weird, Papa," she said and everyone knew it for the compliment that it was. "Where'd you get the skates?" she asked Tom, already removing her shoes. Tom had taught Isabella to skate almost before she could walk.

In those early years of their marriage they had returned to Normal every holiday. Only after the divorce did Norah begin to limit their visits to the summer months. Was that because the memories were too heartbreaking?

"Found them in the attic along with the Christmas decorations," Tom was explaining. "Try these. They're your Aunt Liz's. You might need an extra pair of socks though."

"I'll get a pair," Izzy said and took off.

"Bring an extra for your mother," Tom called as he handed the second pair of skates to Norah. "Seven and a half, right?"

"Right," Norah said, eyeing him suspiciously.

"Clare's an eight—thus, the need for double socks." He handed her the skates.

"All kidding aside," Norah began. "It's Dad's first night home and Mom's exhausted and—"

"And if you weren't here it would be your father's first night home and I would still be tired and we would both settle in to watch our shows and then go to bed," Irene said.

"Your mother's right. You'll do me no favors treating me like a sick old man. Go on. It'll be good for the kid—all that fresh air."

At that moment Izzy came bounding down the stairs and back into the kitchen. She tossed one pair of rolled socks to Norah and sat down and began putting on the second pair. Tom knelt like a shoe salesman and helped her work her foot into one skate.

"How's that feel?" he asked.

"Tight, but I'll get used to it," Izzy said, pulling off the skate and tying the long laces together. She put on her regular shoes then stood and slung the skates over one shoulder. "How do I look?"

"Pretty as one of those Olympic stars," her grandfather said.

"Come on, Mom," she called, heading to the laundry room to get coats, hats and gloves for them both. "It'll be fun."

"I can see that I'm outnumbered," Norah said as she looked at her parents and Tom.

"Yep," her father said. "Might as well face the music."

* * *

They walked the short distance to town. Isabella danced ahead of them catching fat snowflakes on her tongue. Norah filled the space between them with chatter about the church ladies and former schoolmates they had both known. Tom let her talk, knowing it was nerves. What he didn't know was whether her anxious chatter was the product of her fear of skating or—like his—the challenge of separating the life they had once shared here from the separate lives they now lived.

"There's your house," he said. He nodded toward a large Victorian structure that sat on the corner overlooking the square. When they were teenagers the house had been owned by the mayor and his large family. It was always alive with lights in every room in the evenings or with children and dogs rushing in and out during the day. Now it was dark and forlorn, badly in need of paint and repair.

"It looks so sad," Norah said, pausing to look at it. "It's been for sale since the last time I was here. I would have thought someone would have bought it by now. It just needs some TLC."

Tom chuckled. "A *lot* of TLC."

"Why do you think it hasn't sold?" she asked as they pressed on toward the lights and music of the rink.

"According to Dad the recession has hit the town hard. Another plant closed last fall. And the population of the town is aging as younger families move on to other places. That house would be a lot to take on even if it were in great condition."

Norah looked back at it and Tom saw by her expression that she was remembering it the way it had been. "Remember how they used to light that big tree with those little white lights every December?"

"I remember that you used to say that if you owned that house, you'd trim that tree in red, white and blue lights for the Fourth of July. Then as I recall the plan was to take out the blue and use the red and white for Christmas."

"And then take out the white and leave the red for Valentine's," Norah said wistfully.

"Mom! Dad! Come on," Isabella called, already seated on a bench and putting on her skates.

"No guts. No glory," Tom said as he placed his hand on Norah's waist and steered her toward the rink.

Within minutes Isabella had attracted the attention of a group of teens near her age and soon the others were helping her get acclimated to the rhythm of the sport, their laughter like music on the cold night air. Norah envied their ease and spontaneity as they skated to the center of the large makeshift pond.

"Like riding a bicycle," Tom said, watching them as well. "Remember the first time we went skating?" he asked as the two of them glided slowly around the perimeter of the pond.

Norah laughed. "I thought you were going to dump me right then and there, but you were so patient—and I was so…tentative."

"You were a basket case," Tom corrected. "Never in a million years would I ever have guessed that tough little Norah Jenkins might have a hidden phobia about falling down. I mean that was it, wasn't it? It wasn't the ice or the skating per se. It was about not wanting to fall down."

Norah bristled slightly. "Well, people do have their quirks. That was—is mine."

"Is? You mean you never got over it? You were what? Bella's age?"

"I was fifteen and no, I don't believe that you simply outgrow something like that." She eyed the railing that surrounded the pond and saw that he had started to lead them far enough away that it was out of reach. She tightened her grip on his hands.

"Ow!"

"Sorry," she said, glancing at the receding

shore that was solid ground and the security of the railing. "We're getting a little far out."

"We're two feet from the edge and the ice is better here—smoother." She could sense him watching her, felt his arm tighten around her waist. "I'm not going to let you fall, Norah," he promised. "Just trust me, okay?"

There was an edge to his tone. The matter of trust—or the lack thereof on her part—had been a major factor in their divorce. "I am doing what I believe is necessary to secure the future for us and our children," he would argue when she challenged his long hours at work, his absence from home and all the benchmarks of Isabella's first years that he had missed. "You need to trust me on that," he would add.

And Norah would flinch at the implication that he knew what was best for her—the same way she had flinched if anyone suggested such an idea. After their divorce she was the one who had thrown herself into work, telling herself that it was vital that she build a secure career, a secure financial base for her life with Isabella. Not that she ever doubted that Tom would be there for their daughter. He had college covered by the time Izzy was seven. But Norah had been determined to make her way, provide for her child....

"Better?" Tom asked now as they started their second lap around the pond.

Norah nodded and forced herself to relax. But the minute she did, her ankle buckled and she started to fall.

"Got you," Tom assured her, hauling her upright.

"This can't be much fun for you," she said. "Why don't I sit over there and you go get Isabella and skate with her?"

Tom glanced to the center of the ring where Isabella was obviously having a great time with her newfound friends. "I'll make you a deal," he said. "Go one more round with me and I'll buy you hot chocolate and we'll both sit on the sidelines with the rest of the old folks."

"I'm not old," Norah sniffed.

"Do we have a deal or not?"

"Does the hot chocolate come with marshmallows?"

Tom's laugh was filled with pure merriment. It rang across the pond and Norah saw Izzy glance their way and smile. "Come on," he said. "Longer strides—not those short little baby steps. No wonder you fall down. Glide. Glide. Glide. That's better."

Norah could not deny the pure pleasure of sailing along as if her feet had sprouted wings.

She closed her eyes and visualized the grace and beauty of the skaters she'd watched on television. "Don't let go," she begged as she concentrated on following Tom's rhythm.

"Right here, Norah."

There was something in the way he said those words that made Norah open her eyes and look up at him. She searched his face for some underlying meaning, but just then he pulled her closer and spun slowly around. Once again she stiffened and stumbled. This time she fell against his hard chest and felt his arms tighten around her as he lifted her just enough so that her skates were off the ice. "Home base," he said quietly, nodding toward the warming house with the promised hot chocolate.

"Oh. Well, good," she said. "Put me down. I can make it from here."

"And risk having you turn an ankle three days before Christmas? I don't think so," he replied as he scooped her into his arms and glided to the edge.

Over his shoulder Norah saw Izzy headed their way. "Put me down," she urged. "Izzy's coming and she'll take this the wrong way."

Tom shrugged. "She's already seen what she wants to see—no changing that." But he set Norah on the end of a bench and turned to greet their daughter. "Hey, kiddo, I was just getting your mom some hot chocolate. Want some?"

"With marshmallows?"

Tom laughed. "Like mother like daughter. No promises, but I'll ask."

While Tom headed for the warming house, Izzy plopped down next to Norah. "Looked like you and Dad were having fun," she commented, her eyes focused on the other teens.

"I almost fell and your dad was helping me and—"

"Whatever," Izzy replied, dismissing Norah's feeble attempts to explain. "Guess what?" Her eyes brightened and she turned to face Norah directly. "No, I'll wait until Dad comes. I've got a surprise for you both."

"Who are your new friends?"

"You remember Darcy and Heather. They're the sisters who live on the block behind Grandma and Papa. I met them last year at church."

"Oh, that's right. Their mother is the artist, right?"

"And their dad owns the hardware store."

"Hot chocolate with marshmallows," Tom announced as he distributed the steaming cardboard cups.

"Izzy was just telling me about her new friends," Norah said. "And I believe she has some news to share."

Tom sat down on the other side of Isabella and blew on his hot chocolate. "Good news?"

"Good for me—not so good for Darcy and Heather's friend." She glanced from side to side, then stood up and moved to the end of the bench, forcing Norah to slide closer to Tom. "I feel like I'm at a tennis match," she muttered. "There. That's better. Now I can look at you both at the same time." She gave them an innocent grin.

Norah gave her a look of warning that shouted *Stop matchmaking!* which Izzy ignored.

"So the girl who was to play Mary in the church's Christmas Eve pageant fell while skating a couple of days ago. She broke her ankle and banged up her face some. She'll be fine but not by Christmas Eve, so Darcy and Heather asked me if I would do it."

"Do what?" Tom asked.

"Play Mary. Of course, I'd have to rehearse pretty much all day tomorrow, which sort of messes up helping Papa wrap his presents but—"

"I think it's wonderful," Norah interrupted her. "I can help Papa. It'll be like old times—like when I was a kid."

"Dad? Okay?"

Tom set down his cup and held out his arms to her. "It's better than okay. It's great," he said.

"Cool," Izzy said as she buried her face against Tom's shoulder and then pushed away and headed back out onto the ice. "It's a go," she shouted and the teens waiting for her cheered. Izzy turned back. "Oh, and how about I walk home from here with Darcy and Heather? I mean, unless you two want to hang around."

"Nine o'clock curfew," Norah instructed.

"Oh, Mom," Izzy moaned. "Nine-thirty?" she bargained, her eyes shifting to Tom.

"Nine," Tom said firmly.

Once again Tom noticed that Norah was unusually talkative on the way home. She chattered on about everything from how great the new ice rink was for the teens in town, to how much she had always liked Darcy and Heather's parents, to the need to pick up wrapping paper and ribbon the following morning.

"Dad always wants his gifts for Mom to be wrapped in a special way, so it's important to give him a lot of options," she explained as if Tom had questioned the need for more gift wrap.

It dawned on him that she was nervous. And if she was nervous, didn't that mean that maybe she was experiencing some of the same feelings he was? Feelings that perhaps they'd been given this opportunity to take a step back and reexamine past decisions?

Past decisions? Like what?

Tom dismissed the thought as part of the nostalgia of the season and being back in the town where they'd grown up—and fallen in love. He shook off the thought and tried to concentrate on Norah's chatter, but she had fallen silent.

"Look," she said, her voice low as she pointed to the old Victorian house. "Somebody's coming down the front walk."

"That's Keith Olsen, Darcy's dad," Tom said as he picked up the pace. "Keith! Tom Wallace," he said, offering his hand.

"Hey, good to have you home," Keith said, nodding to Norah.

"Are you thinking of buying the mayor's house?" Norah asked, calling the property by the name given to it in its heyday.

Keith laughed. "No. I just check on it now for the bank to make sure there's no broken pipes or vandalism." He glanced back at the dark house. "It's a pity it hasn't sold. Good bones on this one," he observed.

"Can we see it?" Tom asked. *Now where had that come from? He wasn't in the market for a house—certainly not a house in Normal, Wisconsin.* "Not that I'm in the market. It's just I've never been inside and it was a landmark even when we were kids."

"Sure." Keith handed him the key and a large

flashlight. "Just lock up when you leave. You can drop the key and light off at the hardware store tomorrow—coffee's always on."

Chapter Twelve

"I don't believe you did that," Norah said, but her voice was filled with excitement and wonder as they climbed the front stairs to the wraparound porch and the worn front door with its panels of etched glass to either side.

"You don't have to come," he teased.

"Try and keep me out." She held the flashlight while Tom worked the key in the lock and pushed open the door. "Oh, wow!" she whispered reverently as she scanned the light over the broad curved stairway and the wide front foyer.

"They've kept it in good shape," Tom observed. "I would have expected cobwebs and dust bunnies to have taken over by now." He walked across the hall to the double pocket doors that led into the front parlor and pushed them apart.

"Look at that fireplace," Norah said, shining

the light over the decorative tiles that bordered the opening. "And those windows," she added as the moonlight reflecting off the snow spotlighted the large triple window capped by stained-glass panels. The room ran the length of one side of the house. "You could have a television area at one end and a reading and conversation area there," Norah said, mentally arranging furniture.

"Floors need refinishing," Tom observed as he led the way back across the hall to the dining room with its built-in china cabinet, and on to the butler's pantry and the ancient but charming kitchen.

"Look at this," Norah squealed, having made her way back to the front hall. She was standing in a small room to one side of the front door.

"Coat closet?" Tom guessed.

"Ladies' powder room."

"No men allowed?"

"Well, look at it." Norah flashed the light over the wallpaper trimmed with pink roses, the plaster cherubs mounted above the pedestal sink and the ruffled lace skirt of the dressing table.

"You've got a point." He stepped back into the hall and opened a door on the opposite side of the front door. "Ah, separate accommodations," he announced and Norah hurried over to see the men's cloak room complete with wallpaper that featured hunting scenes and furnishings that were decidedly masculine. "Want to go upstairs?"

Four large bedrooms and two bathrooms surrounded the center stairway that continued on to the third floor where they found a large ballroom and three small bedrooms, plus a tiny bathroom near the back stairs that led back down to the kitchen. "Servants?" Norah marveled. "In Normal?"

"It's a big house," Tom observed. "And the mayor and his wife had, what—eight children?"

They walked back down the front stairs, their footsteps silenced by the Oriental runner anchored on each tread with a brass rod. Outside, Norah waited for Tom to lock the door and check to be sure it was secure, then she switched off the flashlight. "That was a real treat," she said. "Thank you."

"If you could buy that place what would you do with it?"

"Oh, I would have—"

"Not when you were a kid. Now." He couldn't imagine why it was important to make the distinction. They were dreaming, after all and weren't the dreams of their youth really all they had when it came to being in this town again?

"I would live in it—with Izzy," Norah replied quietly.

Tom tried to read her expression, but her features were in shadow. "You always missed

living here, didn't you? I mean even before we—
that is, before we decided to split up."

"Just a small-town girl," Norah said with a
laugh. "That's me." They walked along in silence
and then she added, "Seriously, though, I did
think about moving back after you left, but I had
a good job and you'd made sure we had a house."

Tom bristled at her assumption that he was the
one who had left—abandoned the marriage and
his daughter. He reminded himself that she had
credited him with providing them a place to live,
but still the unconscious accusation hurt. "I didn't
want to leave," he said quietly.

Norah looked up at him. "Oh, Tom, I didn't
mean it that way. Of course you didn't. We just—
well, it was a two-way street, right?"

"Would you come back here now?" he asked.

"I've been thinking about it," she admitted.
"Dad's heart attack was a kind of wake-up call.
Even if they're doing all right now, down the road,
they might need more help—more care."

"What about applying for the director's job?"

She shrugged. "I never handed in the application. It's still on my desk. Depending on who
they hire, I might not even have a job."

"You know better than that."

"And I have to think about Izzy," she continued
as if he hadn't spoken. "She's an Arizona girl. Her

friends are there and she's gotten so involved with the church."

"She's thirteen. You need to think about what you want—what you need to be happy."

"I'm happy," Norah protested as they reached her parents' house.

No, you're not really, he thought to himself. He watched Norah go up the porch steps and into the house. *And neither am I.*

The following morning Isabella was up and out early.

"Went to meet the other kids at the church," Irene said when Norah came down for breakfast. "Isn't it wonderful that they've included her in the pageant?"

"It is," Norah agreed. "How's Dad?"

"Dad is fine," Earle boomed from the hallway. "Wondering if he might find an elf around here to help with some wrapping today."

"At your service," Norah said, giving him a bow.

"I could help," Irene offered with a wink at Norah. "But I have some last-minute shopping to do."

"Good," Earle replied. "Do you good to get out of here. You've been hovering like a mother hen ever since I got home from the hospital."

"I'll be here," Norah assured her mother. "You go ahead."

Earle rolled his eyes. "Now let's get one thing straight, Norah. You are helping me wrap presents—not playing nursemaid."

"Got it."

"How was the ice-skating?" Irene asked.

"Oh, Izzy had a lovely time."

"Your mother didn't ask about Isabella," her father said.

"It was fun."

"Did Tom walk you home?"

Norah burst out laughing. "How come suddenly I feel as if we've done a time travel thing and I'm back in high school?"

"It was just a question," Irene huffed as she got up to get more coffee.

"Yes, Mom. Tom and I walked back together and Isabella came later with her friends." She picked at her toast and added. "We ran into Keith Olsen. He was checking the mayor's house."

"That white elephant has been on the market for well over a year," her mother said, shaking her head. "It's so sad. None of the heirs want the place and there it sits, getting older and more decrepit every day."

"Like us," Earle joked.

"It's not so bad," Norah said and did not miss the

way her parents glanced at each other across the breakfast table. "I mean it's well-built and the rooms are so large and lovely. I always loved that house."

"You looked at it?"

"Yeah. Keith let us borrow a flashlight. I'd never been inside."

"You and Tom?"

Norah's head shot up as she realized the thoughts that must be running through her parents' minds. "Now don't go getting the wrong idea. It was pure serendipity."

"If you say so," Earle muttered, but Norah saw him grin at her mother.

"So, Dad, how about we work on getting those gifts wrapped?" Norah didn't wait for an answer as she hurried up the stairs to gather paper, ribbon and trims for the gift-wrapping project. *It was serendipity. Pure coincidence.*

But, oh, what a lovely coincidence it had been. Long after Isabella was asleep, Norah had toured the old house once more in her mind. Room by room she had imagined—as she had when she was a teen—what it might be like to actually live there.

On his way to return the flashlight and keys to Keith at the hardware store, Tom took a real look at his hometown and what he saw was a town redefining itself. Most of his visits to Normal had been brief and if he got into town it was to run errands for his mom. But the unexpected opportunity to have a look inside the mayor's old house had triggered his curiosity.

True, there were still too many vacant storefronts on Main Street and the factory that had been the town's primary employer when he and Norah were growing up had shut down. But other than the mayor's house and one or two others, the homes were occupied, well-tended and not for sale.

He walked past the high school—boarded up and deserted ever since students from Normal had transferred to a larger consolidated high school several miles away. But a large sign in front of the school told of the coming of a trade school and education center in the spring. Everywhere he turned it seemed as if the community was gearing up for rebirth.

Main Street bustled as merchants swept drifted snow away from their front doors, freshened holiday window displays or headed to the post office to pick up the morning mail. He shook off the cold as he pulled open the door to the hardware store. An old-fashioned bell jangled.

"Be right there," Keith called from somewhere in the back.

The heavy door to the loading dock slid shut. "Hey, Tom," Keith called.

"Brought back the key and flashlight."

"Come on back. I was just going to have a cup of tea. There's the promised coffee, but Meredith's got me drinking this green tea. She's gone all healthy on me," he said with a laugh. "Great having you home, Tom," he added.

Normal will always be home. Norah had said that to him more than once in the days when he'd been determined to move them all to California. "Not Arizona," she'd declared, "and certainly not La La Land. That is not who we are, Tom Wallace."

But is it who we have become? He accepted a mug of tea and sat down to visit with Keith. "Town seems to be humming. Is it the holidays or is this normal for Normal?"

"Business has started to pick up. I have to tell you, when the plant closed we all thought we were going to have to go to work for one of the monster stores out near the freeway."

"What happened?"

Keith shrugged. "Some of us got together. Meredith is an artist, you know, and she and some of her colleagues got together and rented space in the old railroad station. They renovated the place and set up galleries and studios there. It's become quite a draw. Then there's the bike trail slash cross-country ski trail. Brings folks into town." He glanced around. "Of course, we've got a ways to go yet, but it's a good time to be living here."

A customer came in and Keith excused himself. Tom sipped his tea and listened to the exchange between Keith and his customer, the sound of someone calling out to a neighbor from the street, the honk of a car horn that sounded more friendly than irritated as it would have in California. Everything about the place throbbed with possibility.

Keith's words echoed through Tom's mind as he picked out some new lights for the tree at his parents' house and added a special ornament for his mom.

"Ever think about coming back?" Keith asked as he rang up the sale.

"Haven't you ever heard the old adage about not being able to go home again?"

Keith handed him his receipt. "That's just a book title. The town could use a good lawyer—and social workers are always in demand," he added.

"Norah and I are…"

Keith shrugged. "It's not like they carve divorce papers in stone, you know. Every couple goes through rough patches. You and Norah— well, everybody was stunned to hear you two had split up."

Made for each other. That's how the locals used

to talk about them. "Me too," Tom muttered and realized Keith had heard him.

"Like I said, nothing's carved in stone."

That idea stayed with Tom as he helped his Dad set the large Douglas fir into the stand and position it in front of the bay window.

"They're here," his mom called from the hall and hurried to open the front door to welcome Isabella, Norah and her parents.

For all the years that their parents had been friends they had shared the tradition of trimming each other's trees together. In fact Tom had proposed to Norah one night after they had trimmed the tree at her house and they had shared the news the following night when everyone was gathered at his house. There had been so many shared moments like that. How many more were they likely to have? Earle's heart attack had been more than a health scare—it had been a real wake-up call for all of them.

He watched as his dad hugged Bella and then Norah, saw his mom wrap her arm around Bella's shoulder and lead her toward the kitchen. Heard Norah's parents protest that they couldn't possibly eat another bite having just finished supper as they followed his parents down the hall. And there was Norah. She was standing uncertainly in the doorway looking at the giant tree.

"Wow!"

"Yeah," Tom replied. "Can we say overkill? We already had to cut six inches off the bottom, but Mom was adamant that this was the one."

"It's beautiful and smells fabulous. Like—well, like Christmas," she said, laughing as she ventured farther into the room.

"Help me get these lights on it. I want to surprise Mom," Tom said as he unwrapped the packages he bought from Keith.

"Oh, look at them. Snowmen and candles and—oh, this one is wonderful. Little trees and poinsettias."

"Keith had a good selection." *Good time to be living here. Nothing's carved in stone. Made for each other.* Tom plugged in the lights and started draping them on the tree. "Do you ever think about coming back here—to stay, Norah?"

"I hadn't until…."

"Yeah, your dad has always seemed indestructible to me."

"I think about being their only child—I mean your folks have you and your sisters, but…"

"Oh, Tommy!" Eleanor squealed. "What lovely lights!"

Just before noon on Christmas Eve Isabella kicked off her boots on the mat in the laundry room and shrugged out of her ski jacket, scarf and mittens. "Mom?" She spotted a folded note on the kitchen table.

> Gone with Grandma to help decorate the church. Papa is napping. Lunch in the fridge. Love, Mom

The phone rang and she hurried to grab it before it could wake her grandfather. "Hello?"

"Isabella? Is that you?" Stan Morrison's gravelly voice was unmistakable and usually welcomed, but Isabella had the strangest feeling she wasn't going to like what he had to say.

"Hi, Dr. Morrison."

"How's everything up there in the north woods? Have you got a white Christmas?"

"Fine. Yes. Mom's not here."

"Oh, well, ask her to give me a call, would you?"

"Could I take a message?"

"Sure. Let her know we found her application. I guess in all the trauma of hearing about her dad—how is he anyway?"

"He's doing just fine, thank you," Isabella said, her mind racing with the fact that in spite of her mother, the application had been found. What did that mean?

"That's good. Well, might as well say this outright—kind of an early Christmas present. Let her know we've considered the applications—all of them—and the job is hers if she wants it. We're going to close up early since it's Christmas Eve, but I'll be at home. Have her call me, okay?"

"Yes, sir. Thank you."

"Merry Christmas, Isabella."

"Happy New Year," Isabella added automatically before placing the phone back on its charger. Her lunch forgotten, she paced the downstairs of the house. She paused in front of the tree that they had all decorated the night before, just after doing the same thing at her other grandparents'. What a fun day it had been. So filled with memories and stories triggered by the ornaments—stories about her dad as a boy, her mom when she was Isabella's age, the two of them the year they got engaged and Isabella's first Christmas. And best of all had been the way her parents and grandparents had all laughed together and teased each other—like a real family.

Her cell rang and Isabella grabbed it.

"Hey," Darcy said without preamble. "Heather and I are going to town for some last-minute shopping. Wanna come?"

She could tell her Mom about the call later. "Sure."

"Fifteen minutes," Darcy replied and rang off.

* * *

The church was electric with anticipation, from the children gathered in the hallway behind the altar to parents, friends and neighbors crowded into the pews. Angel wings got caught on shepherds' crooks while mothers tied bathrobes and straightened foil-covered cardboard crowns. It was Christmas Eve in Normal, Wisconsin, and a tradition that went back to before Norah was born was about to begin—the annual reenactment of the Nativity story.

Isabella peeked out from behind the burlap backdrop that served as the stable. "There's Dad," she said excitedly, "and the grands—all sitting together. They've saved you a seat on the end," she told Norah. "Right next to Dad," she added with a mischievous grin.

"I brought you something," Norah said, ignoring her daughter's last comment. She unfolded a woven rose-colored shawl as light as air as she floated it up and over Izzy's long hair. "Your grandmother and I thought this would be exactly what Mary might choose," she explained as she arranged one end over Izzy's shoulder and then adjusted the edges to frame Izzy's face.

"Oh, Mom, it's beautiful," Izzy exclaimed. "Darcy, look," she called to her friend who was going over her part as narrator for the evening's performance.

"Perfect," Darcy said.

"Thanks, Mom. I love it." She threw her arms around Norah and added, "I love you."

"Places!" Darcy's mom called and Norah gave Izzy a final squeeze and sent her on her way.

The Christmas Eve service was a wonderful symphony of all that reminded worshippers of life's true blessings. The children—some of them not more than four or five years old—played their parts to perfection. Darcy was the perfect narrator, her strong precise voice giving fresh interpretation to the timeless scripture. But when Izzy came down the aisle, Norah heard Tom's breath catch and she knew that he was probably thinking the same thing she was. Their daughter was growing up, evolving into a lovely young woman and in the blink of an eye they might find themselves in a church somewhere watching her come down another aisle toward a young man waiting at the altar.

It seemed the most natural thing in the world to slide her hand into Tom's as they stood beside each other singing an old carol while Izzy took her place at the altar and gently laid a doll in the manger. The pageant played out and the service moved on to its final moments—the lighting of the candles everyone had been given upon their arrival. At the far end of their pew the usher lit Eleanor's candle. She turned to Tom's father and he in turn lit Irene's and so it went until it was Tom who turned to Norah. He steadied her hand as he bent the flame of his lighted candle to hers.

And when she looked up and into Tom's eyes, Norah felt a kind of peace come over her, a sense that in this moment her life had taken a turn for the better. They would be all right. Whatever the future held, they were once again the friends they had been from the first day they had met at this very church. It was that friendship she had missed most of all, that one person she knew she could go to with anything—no matter how ridiculous or far-fetched it might seem.

There was a short reception following the service before everyone headed home to enjoy the rest of Christmas Eve with family and close friends. Norah couldn't help noticing how quiet Isabella became on the ride home.

"Are you feeling all right, Izzy?"

"Sure."

The smile was too bright, the single word answer way too chipper. Norah placed the back of her hand on Izzy's cheek. No obvious fever. "You did a terrific job tonight."

"Thanks."

"Best Mary I've ever seen and I've been going to that pageant for over fifty years," Norah's dad assured her.

"Oh, Papa, I bet you said the same thing when Mom played Mary."

Her grandmother laughed. "She knows you too well, Earle."

"Can we open a present tonight?" Izzy asked as they pulled into the garage.

"It's tradition," Irene said. "But first we need to put out some milk and cookies for Santa and some carrots for his reindeer."

"Oh, Grandma," Izzy giggled.

"What? You don't believe in Santa?" Papa said. "You do realize that those who stop believing no longer get presents?"

"I believe. I believe," Izzy shouted as they all crowded into the laundry room to remove their outer garments and boots.

They were just opening the traditional one present—the ones from Norah's Aunt Helen who lived in Florida—when there was a knock at the back door.

"Just me," Tom called.

"Too bad," Earle replied. "We had our hearts set on Santa being early."

"Well, I brought a few more packages for under the tree."

"For me?" Izzy squealed as she took the gift-wrapped boxes from him and examined the tags. "Ooh, Mom, this one's for you." She held up a box and rattled it vigorously.

"Stop that," Norah said, but she was laughing as she took the package and shook it gently. "Something to wear," she guessed.

"Who's it from?" Izzy asked, her eyes on her father.

"To Norah, Love Eleanor and Dan," Norah quoted. "Ah, that's so nice." She placed the package under the tree, then relieved Izzy of the rest of the gifts and added them to the pile. "You, young lady, have had a very full couple of days. Time for bed."

"Dad?"

"You heard your mother. Hey, how about having an early breakfast with me in the morning and letting these old folks sleep in?"

"Can Mom come?"

"No, you go with your dad. It'll be fun—a new tradition," Norah hurried to say. The truth was that there had already been so much togetherness that she was very afraid that Izzy's dreams of a true reconciliation were working overtime. Besides, she still wanted to talk to Izzy about the possibility of them moving permanently to Normal.

Tom studied Norah for a second, then grinned at Isabella. "Like I said, let's let the old folks sleep in. Just you and me, kid."

"Okay. Eight?"

"Seven," Tom said and everyone laughed when Isabella groaned. "Best time," he assured her.

"Then I'm going to bed," she announced. "Merry Christmas—" she paused on the stairway and raised one hand dramatically "—and God bless us, every one."

"Well, speaking of bedtime," Irene said, "Earle, it's well past yours. We've got a busy day tomorrow." She flicked her eyes toward Tom and Norah.

Earle yawned and stretched. "Be sure you turn out the tree lights, Norah."

"Good night," Norah and Tom said in unison.

Left alone with Tom, Norah was suddenly shy. "Sorry about that. Everyone seems to be match-making these days."

"They mean well," Tom said. He stood in front of the tree for a long moment while Norah scurried about, clearing away the wrappings from the gifts the family had opened earlier. "Well, I'd better let you get some rest as well."

"Do you have a minute?" Norah asked.

Tom looked taken aback but pleased. He took a seat on the sofa that faced the tree and patted the space beside him. "I always have time for you, Norah."

She perched on the edge of the sofa and pressed her fingers over the fabric of a throw pillow. "I don't know where to start," she said with a nervous laugh.

"Can't help you there. What's this about?"

She looked at him. "It's about something Dad said about me marking time ever since—well, for a while now." She took a deep breath and plunged in. "Tom, what would you think about the idea of Izzy and me moving back here—to Normal?"

"I'd start by asking you why you might do that," he answered, his eyes riveted on hers.

Norah stood and paced the small area between the sofa and the tree, pausing every now and then to reposition an ornament or light. "It's a terrible idea, right? I mean, I have a good job in Arizona and a house and Izzy has her friends and her life there. I mean, what would I do here?"

"Okay, you've given me reasons why not to do it. What about the other side of the argument?"

"Once a lawyer," she murmured and Tom shrugged. "First, there's Mom and Dad."

"Get back to what Earle said—about 'marking time.'"

"He struck a chord," Norah admitted. "After—when you and I—went our separate ways, all of my energy was focused on Isabella. Making sure she was happy. Making sure things stayed as normal as possible for her. And even after time passed and she moved on—I didn't."

"What about your work? That's important."

"It's not what it was. The focus changed. My role in it changed. I went there to make a real difference, but lately—"

"That was Luke's doing. He's gone now. Maybe when the new person takes over—"

Norah shrugged and turned back to the tree.

"What else?"

"Izzy," Norah replied. "How can I expect her to just pull up stakes and move here? Normal is my hometown, not hers."

"Maybe you should ask her how she'd feel about it," Tom suggested.

"Would you? I mean, would you feel her out maybe tomorrow when you two have breakfast? Just raise a what-if situation? Then if she was totally turned off, I'd have my answer."

"And based on that you'd go back to Arizona to a job that no longer inspires you? And what about Irene and Earle?"

Norah sighed. "I know. Maybe I could get them to move to Phoenix." She saw by Tom's expression that such an idea didn't even merit a comment. She collapsed back onto the sofa, hugging the throw pillow to her.

"Hey," Tom said, gently removing the pillow and putting his arm around her shoulders. "Let's not get the sleigh before the reindeer here. Let me feel out Bella in the morning and then you can decide your next step."

Norah sighed with relief and allowed her head to drop onto Tom's shoulder. "Thank you," she murmured.

"Want to know what I think?" he asked, tightening his hold on her.

Norah looked up at him and nodded.

"I think it's a good idea," he whispered and kissed her forehead.

"You have no idea what that means to me," she said and curled her feet under her as she snuggled more securely into the curve of his arm. "This has been a good Christmas, Tom."

"It's not over yet," he reminded her with a chuckle.

Suddenly she sat up. "You didn't get me anything, did you? I mean ever since we—since the divorce—we've never—you didn't?"

Tom shrugged. "Seems like we're moving on to a new plateau. I thought a gift was a good marker for that."

"But I didn't get anything for you and now it's after midnight and all the stores are closed and—"

Tom touched a finger to her lips. "You have given me your trust," he said.

"You always had that. Well, maybe not *always,* but certainly when it comes to Izzy."

"Okay, then. Just remember you're the one with the need to match me gift for gift," he said and before she could respond, he leaned over and kissed her.

Not just a holiday peck on the lips, but he pulled her into his arms and kissed her with all of the passion they had shared as teenagers. A kiss that left her stunned, breathless and wanting more.

"There," he said, setting her gently away from him and standing. "Now we're even."

She blinked up at him as he reached under the tree and handed her a heavy shoebox-sized package. "My present to you," he said. "Afraid it doesn't quite measure up to that kiss, but as you used to say 'it's not a contest,' so Merry Christmas."

He waited while she opened it. Inside was a pair of ice skates with double blades—the kind children wear when learning to skate. "Got you the training wheels model," he said with a grin.

Norah laughed. "They're perfect. Thank you."

He held out his hand to her and she walked with him to the door. "Be sure Bella is up for our breakfast," he said. "I'll talk to her."

Norah nodded and pulled open the front door. "Thanks, Tom—for everything." She stood on tiptoe and kissed his cheek and when he looked surprised, she indicated the sprig of fresh mistletoe her mother had hung over the doorway. "Merry Christmas," she called as he headed down the front walk. "I…"

Tom turned and looked back at her, but she waved him away and closed the door. She leaned against the door and realized that she had almost added, "I love you."

Chapter Thirteen

Isabella barely slept. If she had been younger and still believed in the magic of Santa and his reindeer, her insomnia might be understandable. The truth was that Darcy's invite to go shopping had given her all the excuse she needed to put the call from Dr. Morrison out of her mind. Of course, she had remembered it several times through the evening but convinced herself the timing wasn't right to blurt out that her mother had been offered the director's job.

Face it, she thought as she pulled on jeans, a bulky turtleneck sweater sent by Aunt Helen and heavy socks, *you found every reason not to tell her.* She glanced at the other twin bed where her mother was sleeping, her mouth slightly open, her eyelids twitching with dreams. *You don't want to tell her because that would mean it's all decided. You and Mom will go back to Phoenix and Dad will go back to California, and maybe by the time you get out of high school, the two of them will finally realize they were meant for each other.*

She tiptoed to the door and slowly turned the knob. The smell of fresh brewed coffee wafted up the stairs and she heard her father's familiar laughter and the clatter of a spoon in a ceramic mug. It was so good being here—almost like being a real family again. Sometimes with just Mom and her in Arizona, it seemed really lonely.

"Merry Christmas," she said as she entered the kitchen and kissed her grandmother's cheek. Grandma was still in her bathrobe—last year's model—and slippers, but Isabella's dad was dressed for the snowy morning.

"Ready?" he said as he drained the last of his coffee.

"Sure, but nothing's open, so maybe Grandma's oatmeal wouldn't be terrible. I mean, it would be great," she amended, seeing her grandmother's look of mock offense.

"Nope. You'll have to settle for day-old bagels and a thermos of hot chocolate. We're going on a breakfast picnic."

"Uh, Dad, it's like freezing out there?"

"So bundle up." He kissed Irene's cheek. "I'll have her back by nine," he promised.

"Take your time," she said. "Have fun."

Tom pulled an extra wool scarf off a hook in the back hall and wrapped it several times around Isabella's neck until it covered her chin, then he plopped an old knitted toboggan on her head.

"Dad!" Isabella protested, "I look like a dork."

"This is not a fashion moment," he declared and pulled open the back door. "Your chariot awaits," he added, pointing to a large sled.

Isabella giggled as she sat on the sled and pulled the blanket Tom handed her over her legs and knees. "Mush!" she cried.

Tom picked up the sled rope and pulled her across the yard and on into the woods behind her grandparents' house. "Oops," he said as they came to an open space that overlooked a frozen pond below. "Here's the dilemma," he announced scratching his head as if he hadn't set up this whole thing. "Breakfast is down there and we're up here and I don't know about you but I am starving. If only there were some way to get down there faster."

"Oh, Dad, do not pretend you didn't plan this whole thing. Come on." She scooted forward and wrapped the blanket around her shoulders as Tom positioned the sled on the brink of the hill. Then he climbed on behind her, pulled her tight against himself.

"Ready?"

"Set! Go!" Isabella cried raising her arms high and shouting with joy as they flew down the hill.

The sled came to a stop several feet from the edge of the pond and a rattan picnic basket. "Breakfast is served, my lady." He pulled out the thermos, two cups, cloth napkins, and bagels sandwiched around cream cheese and Grandma Eleanor's famous peach jam.

"Heavenly," Isabella sighed as she took the first bite.

They sat straddling the ends of the sled using the middle as a table between them. "So, talk to me," her dad said.

"About?"

"Whatever's on your mind—Christmas, the pageant last night, your mom, whatever."

Isabella felt her throat tighten. "Can't we just enjoy the morning?" she said quietly and feigned an interest in the silent woods in the distance. Without warning the tears came. Isabella tried to sniff them back, pretend they were from the cold, not her culpability in keeping Dr. Morrison's news a secret.

"Hey, what's this? Has something happened?"

She sighed. Dad would know what to do. "Dr. Morrison called yesterday."

"Oh."

"Yeah. He found Mom's application and he's offering her the job."

"Is she going to accept it?"

"She doesn't know. I never gave her the message."

"I see."

"At first I forgot—truly. Darcy called and well, anyway I forgot. But then I remembered."

"And still didn't tell her?"

"I remembered when we got to the church and she was there with Grandma Eleanor finishing up the decorations and I had to get ready for the pageant and it just seemed like the wrong time."

"Okay, but there was time later."

Isabella ducked her head. "I know. But we were having so much fun and it felt so—like a real family and I just—"

"You have to tell her, Bella."

"I know."

"You should be proud of her—happy for her. She's worked hard for this."

"I'm proud of her. It's just if she takes this—and why wouldn't she? It's just we'll all be back where we were—us in Phoenix, you in San Francisco."

Tom lifted her face to his. "Honey, us all being here isn't the real world," he said. "It's wonderful but—well, it's more like a wonderful accident, a kind of special gift."

"Exactly," Isabella argued. "It's as if God brought us here. Admittedly Papa's heart attack was maybe overkill, but we're here. There's a reason for that—a plan in action."

"Bella, are you saying you could live here—permanently?"

"It wouldn't be terrible."

"But Mom's been offered the job she's always wanted."

Isabella made a face.

"Maybe we're becoming a holiday family—no more splitting time between us. We could do all the holidays together. I'll bet she would go for that."

"So, I have to tell her about the call." It was a statement not a question.

"Yeah, and the sooner the better."

Isabella packed up their picnic and stood up, her back to her father. "I was just so sure that God had this plan for us to be together." Her shoulders shook and Tom was on his feet with his arms around her in seconds. That brought on the full flood of tears. "Why can't we be a real family?" she wailed.

"We are," he assured her. "Hey, glass half-full, remember? Think about all the progress we've made in just a few short weeks. Don't spoil what's left of our time together by looking at the dark side, honey. We're sharing Christmas and then New Year's—that's a huge step forward, Bella."

She looked up at him and smiled. "I guess when you look at it that way. Okay, let's go. I'll tell her as soon as we get back—right after we open the presents—" She saw her father's frown and sighed. "As soon as we get back."

Isabella wasn't the only one who had spent a restless night. It wasn't visions of sugarplums dancing in Norah's head. It was her father's heart attack, the aging of both parents, the draw she felt to be there for them, and more than she was willing to admit, the draw she had been feeling toward being back in Normal.

And it's Tom.

She tried to tell herself that the season with all its memories and good tidings of peace and joy had created a false sense of what might have been. But the truth was from the moment she had gotten the call about her father's heart attack, her first instinct had been to turn to Tom. No, it had really started with Denver and Izzy getting sick. And then later when she'd needed to talk to someone about Izzy's change in attitude, it had been perfectly natural to call Tom. After all, it was how they had always handled things with bringing up Isabella.

But when she had decided to contact him about her résumé and the idea of applying for the new job, something had clicked into place like a puzzle piece that had once seemed impossible and then slid into place so perfectly. And even though she told herself that the way they were interacting with one another now that they were here in Normal had to do with not wanting to upset their parents or Izzy, the truth was it felt so right—so absolutely genuine.

"Mom?"

When Izzy returned. Norah was sitting up in bed. She grinned at her daughter's red cheeks and nose. "Dad did a picnic?" she guessed.

"Like at the bottom of this giant sledding hill," Izzy giggled. "He is so weird sometimes."

Norah saw that statement for the compliment it was. She held back the covers and patted the bed beside her. "Come on. Warm up with me, then we'll go rip through all those presents."

Izzy snuggled in next to her. Norah wrapped one arm around her daughter and pulled her close. "That's nice," she said.

"I have to tell you something, Mom, and I don't want you to get mad or upset. I mean, you couldn't have done anything about it with today being Christmas and all so—"

"What's happened?"

"Dr. Morrison called—yesterday. He found your application and you've got the job. Congratulations."

"What!" Norah tried digesting this flood of information. "You mean they want to interview me?"

"Nope. He said if you want it the job's yours." Izzy looked directly at her for the first time since blurting out the news. In her eyes Norah saw a message that was even more unsettling than the fact she had the job.

Please, don't, Izzy's eyes seemed to plead.

"Wow," Norah murmured. "Well, that's something, isn't it?"

"Yeah." Izzy slid off the bed.

"Something for us to consider," Norah added and saw Izzy freeze. "See, I was going to talk to you about something today once we'd gotten through the gift opening and church and Christmas dinner. But maybe now's the best time."

"For what?" Izzy stared out the window.

"I've been thinking maybe we could consider moving back here, Izzy."

"Here? In this house?"

"No. In Normal—in a house or apartment of our own."

Izzy turned. Her eyes were enormous. "What about the job?"

"That does bring a new element to the discussion," Norah acknowledged. "But we have to consider everything, After all it would be a big change. This isn't Phoenix. It's much smaller and it gets cold here and—"

"Let's do it." Izzy clapped her hands with delight, then hopped onto her own bed and started listing the pluses. "We'd be near both sets of grands. I could help them. Oh, and we're not that far away from Minnesota so maybe MJ could come for a weekend or I could go there. And there's Darcy and Heather and—"

"Slow down," Norah warned. "Take some time to think it over. We don't need to make a decision right this minute. It's just an option."

There was a loud knock at the door and Earle called out. "You girls decent?"

"Come in, Dad," Norah called and put a finger to her lips to warn Izzy not to say anything about them possibly moving just yet. Izzy nodded and flung herself at her grandfather. "Oh, Papa, this is just going to be the best Christmas ever. Let's go open presents."

They made short work of the pile of gifts, ate a second breakfast and then piled in the car for church services traditionally held at noon on Christmas Day. While the evening before the sanctuary had hummed with excitement and conversation, on Christmas Day everyone entered in silence. They might nod and smile at neighbors and friends, but no one spoke as the old pipe organ belted out carols and the scent of fresh evergreens, and dozens of lit candles filled the air. Everyone was dressed in the festive colors of the season and a mantle of love and serenity seemed to cover every shoulder, fill every heart.

Norah sat with her parents and Izzy in one of the side pews. She glanced around and saw that Tom and his parents had not yet arrived and every pew was nearly filled. Just then she spotted them standing at the back of the church. Tom smiled at her and time stood still. How many times in this very church had she thought of Tom only to look up and see him there, smiling at her, watching her?

As his parents hurried down the opposite aisle and took their places with the rest of the choir seated in the side pews, Tom raised one eyebrow at Norah. She nodded and then pressed closer to Izzy so Tom could squeeze in with them.

The hour-long service consisted of a series of responsive readings, choir anthems and organ solos that served as background for silent prayer and meditation. Norah was surprised to find that these times for prayer came as naturally to her as breathing. Maybe it was being back in the church of her youth. And maybe Izzy was right. God was reaching out to her—or more likely she was reaching out to God.

Dear God, thank you for the wealth of blessings you have bestowed on our families—for health restored and for bringing us all together here at times in our individual lives when we truly need the support and caring of each other. Please help us to make the right decisions as we go forward. We all know what Isabella wants. Over these last weeks so much has changed for us. Izzy believes Your hand is guiding all of that. Forgive me, but I'm not that sure. Please don't let her heart be broken again. Please help me—and Tom—see what's real and what's fantasy. It is blessing enough that we have found our way back to being friends. Help us show our beloved daughter that sometimes friendship is enough—help me accept that it can be enough.

Norah swallowed. The truth hit her. In her heart of hearts she hoped Izzy was right and that God did intend for her to be with Tom again. She was in love with him, had always loved him, would always love him. It was not Izzy who needed to come to terms with the idea that friendship might be the extent of it—it was Norah.

Help me, she silently prayed. *Open my eyes. Show me Your way.*

The organ music swelled to a crescendo and the congregation rose as one for the final carol, "Joy to the World."

Tom sang with gusto as if he believed every word, as if he had suddenly recognized the truth of every word. Norah felt her heart open to the sheer beauty of the moment. The three of them a family again if only for these few days. She would talk to Tom about the job in Phoenix versus the idea of moving back to Normal. She trusted him. Oh, how she had missed being able to talk about things like this with him.

"…and heaven and nature sing," she bellowed so loud that Tom and Izzy both looked at her and grinned.

"I think moving back here is a great idea," Tom said that afternoon as they walked back to her house after both families had shared a traditional brunch at the home of Tom's parents. "It's good for Irene and Earle. For Isabella. Not so sure it's the best thing for you."

"How so?"

"You've practically built the program at the agency. This would be your chance to really do the things you've always wanted to do there."

Norah shrugged. "Maybe I've been a little too invested in my work," she said. "Maybe Luke did me a favor that day when he tried to fire me. It certainly made me look at the job in a new way."

"But Luke's not part of this anymore."

"It doesn't matter. It occurred to me that trying to find your identity in the work you do is at best a moving target."

"You don't need to find your identity," Tom argued. "You're you."

Norah stopped walking and looked up at him. "And who is that?" she said quietly. "Once I was your wife. Then I was Izzy's mom. Then I was whatever my title of the moment was at the agency. I've been a lot of things to a lot of people, but who is Norah?"

"And you think coming back here is the right place to find answers?"

"It feels—safe. It feels familiar."

"You can't turn back the clock, Norah."

"Sure you can," she said half-jokingly. "We do it every fall when we go off daylight saving time."

But Tom remained serious. "You know what I'm saying."

"I know. I'm not going into this with blinders on," she assured him. "I know the difference between being Izzy's age and growing up here and the realities of making a life here. I'll have to find work and there are bound to be moments when Izzy—and I—think we made the wrong choice."

"Want my best advice?" He placed her hand in the crook of his arm.

"That was the point of sending the others ahead and walking home with you," she said with a smile.

"Okay, here it comes. Don't turn down the job in Phoenix yet. Call Morrison and tell him you'll have a decision when you get back after New Year's. Then while you're here explore what the reality of moving back here might be—check out job opportunities, schools, housing, the works."

"That sounds like a wonderful plan. Izzy is ready to put a down payment on a house, but you're right. We need the whole picture."

"Okay, so now that we've solved that, I had an idea." He told her of his idea that going forward they would spend all holidays together. "Either here or in San Francisco—or Phoenix if you decide to go back. We could maybe travel some—springbreak in Washington so Izzy gets a taste of her nation's capital. What do you think?"

Norah laughed. "Oh, Tom, I thought it was just Izzy and me who were getting caught up in the fantasy of the holiday. Do you know what you're proposing? I mean what if you want to spend a holiday with someone else?"

"Who else?"

"A girlfriend?"

Tom shrugged and grinned. "I'll bring her along and you'll bring your guy. If they can't handle it, then they aren't the right ones. Let's be a family—at least to the extent we can be."

It had always amazed Norah how Tom could take the most complex situation and winnow it down to the simplest terms. It was one of the things she had loved most about him. And, she couldn't help remembering, it was also one of the things that had left her stunned and furious when he had left her.

She glanced up at him as he opened the front door to her parents' house and waited for her to precede him.

"Are you happy, Tom?"

He seemed surprised at the question. "Of course."

But the answer had come automatically and the assurance in his smile did not reach his eyes. She touched his cheek.

"You mean in general?" Tom shrugged. "This isn't about me." He kissed her fingers. "You're doing the right thing, Norah. Take your time. Gather the facts. Then decide."

"And in the meantime?" Norah couldn't seem to take her eyes off his fingers entwined with hers. "Will you help me make sure Izzy doesn't get her hopes too high? I mean, she's likely to see this as the next step in God's grand plan—for us."

"I can't stop her from praying for what she's always wanted, Norah."

"In church today it occurred to me that maybe we're the ones who should be seeking God's guidance."

"Great minds," he tapped her forehead and then his own. "I was praying hard during those silent meditations this morning."

Norah was surprised. "Me too," she admitted. "Think it's possible for two former holiday-only churchgoers to change?"

"It's worth a shot—when we were teens we were pretty into our faith."

"Like Izzy," Norah said.

"And a little child shall lead them?" He wrapped his arm around her shoulders. "Don't sell yourself short, Norah. You've raised a fabulous kid. You've built a career you can be proud of, and yet you're still thinking about coming back here for your parents' sake."

"Don't put me up for sainthood yet," Norah cautioned. "Starting fresh has some really selfish appeal to me right now." She looked up at him. "I don't want to some day look back at my life and have the best I can say about it is that I made do."

Tom pulled her to him and hugged her. "Lady, you may be many things but selfish is not on the list, okay? In fact, I would applaud selfish. For once in your life make a decision based on what's best for you. Isabella will be fine whatever you decide."

"Thanks," she whispered as she hugged him back and drew strength from his embrace. *If only*... She pulled away a little. "How about a turkey sandwich?"

He grinned and then kissed her.

"Tom!" she protested when he broke the kiss.

He grinned and pointed to the mistletoe. "Blame your mom," he said and headed down the hall toward the kitchen.

"We should have a New Year's Eve party," Isabella announced as they sat around the kitchen table later that night picking at the remains of their supper.

"What a good idea," Irene agreed. "Why don't you start a guest list, Isabella, and then we can plan a menu."

"And games," Isabella said.

"Parlor games," Earle said.

"Oh, stop sounding like you were born in Victorian times," Irene chastised him but she was laughing.

"How about a scavenger hunt?" Isabella suggested. "Scavenger hunt and then all meet at the church for midnight services, then come back here and see who found the most things on their list and eat dessert and—"

"And by that time it'll be nearly time for breakfast," her grandfather teased her. "Might as well not go to bed at all."

Izzy eyes and smile widened. "We could watch the sunrise—the dawning of the first day of a new year—cool!"

"Well, I can see I'd better rest up for this grand affair," Earle said. "Come on, Renie, let these young folks clear away. That holiday movie you like is on the family channel—starts in five minutes. Want to snuggle up in bed and watch it with me?"

Irene smiled and pulled off her apron. "Now how could I possibly refuse an offer like that?"

"I'm going to call Darcy and Heather," Isabella said. "It's okay to invite them and their parents, right?"

"It's fine, but don't get too ambitious with your guest list," Norah warned. "It's not that big of a house."

Izzy frowned as she scanned the living room and small dining room visible through the kitchen pass-through. "Yeah, that could be a problem." And she was off, cell phone already to her ear as she bolted up the stairs and shut the door to the bedroom she and Norah were sharing.

"I should go," Tom said.

"Oh no you don't." Norah tossed him the dish towel. "You're not leaving me alone to clear up this mess. I'll wash. You wipe."

"They have this marvelous invention called a dishwasher."

Norah pulled open the dishwasher door to show him it was already filled. "Unless you want to add unloading this to clearing up?"

"I'll wipe," he said as he stacked plates and flatware and carried them to the sink. "Remember that first apartment in Arizona?"

"Yeah. We could barely turn around in that kitchen."

"But it was fun. We had some good times in that place."

"Seems like a long time ago." Norah handed him a plate and he wiped it dry and put it in the cupboard. His actions brought back memories of nights spent washing dishes in that first apartment, nights when they had talked about the future—their future. *You can't go back—only forward.* "Last plate," she announced brightly and handed it to him as she drained the water and wiped out the sink. Their chore completed, there was an awkward silence in the kitchen.

"Well…" Tom said, making the first move. Norah followed him into the front hall and waited by the door while he put on his jacket and gloves. "See you tomorrow?"

Hundreds of times when they were in high school and college they had stood in this very place. He had asked the same question. She had made the same reply, "Sure."

She pulled open the front door and made sure she stood well out of range of the mistletoe. It had been an emotional roller coaster of a day. One more kiss—even a "mistletoe peck" as Tom had once called it—would put her over the edge. Tom glanced at the mistletoe and her position and laughed. "Coward."

Chapter Fourteen

The next day Norah searched various Web sites for job postings. While there were some possibilities in the Madison area, that would mean an hour's commute each way—unless she and Izzy moved closer to Madison.

"But then what's the point?" Izzy said with maddening logic. "I mean, isn't the idea to be closer to the grands?"

"We would be. Just not in the same town."

"So you're talking really starting over—like totally?" She flopped onto the sofa. "I mean here at least I've got some friends and the church youth group and—"

"Don't get ahead of yourself," Norah said, fighting to keep her own frustration out of her voice. "Nothing's been decided, okay?"

"What about a place to live? Does that look any better?"

"First I need to find gainful employment."

"Hey, what about that cool old house you like so much?"

"The mayor's mansion? Oh, Izzy, we could never afford that and even if we could, it would need a ton of work and it's a huge house for just the two of us."

"We could turn it into a bed and breakfast," Izzy suggested, her eyes alive with what she clearly saw as the brilliance of that suggestion.

"We could," Norah said as if she might seriously consider the idea. "So you're saying that you would be willing to make beds and clean guest rooms and bathrooms for tourists while I cook them elaborate breakfasts and prepare afternoon tea—assuming we have guests?"

Izzy made a face. "We could hire help?"

Norah shook her head.

"Okay, bad idea. You're not that good of a cook anyway," she reasoned.

"Isabella Wallace," Norah protested, but she was laughing because it was true. Tom had been the better cook. She wondered if he still tried new recipes from time to time. *You could ask him,* she realized and felt a warm spot in her heart because Tom was right down the street, not halfway across the country.

"We could at least look at the place," Izzy was saying. "Come on, Mom. Let's just look at it. It'll be fun—and educational for me to see a house like that."

"It would also be a waste of time—and time is not something we have a lot of right now. Besides don't you have things you need to do for the party?"

The phone rang and Norah grabbed it before Izzy could. "Go," she whispered to her daughter before greeting the caller.

"Norah? Meredith Olsen."

"Hi."

"I hope I'm not out of line here, but it's a small town as I'm sure you know and news tends to travel fast." She paused for a breath and added, "Is it true you're thinking of moving back?"

"How did you know?"

"I was in the chair next to Irene at Sadie's this morning."

After Tom had left the evening before, Norah had stopped by her parents' room and told them she was thinking about coming home to Normal. Her mother had gone to the hairdresser earlier that morning and Sadie Evanston's shop had always been gossip central.

"Isabella and I are thinking about it," Norah admitted.

"Great. Irene said you were checking out jobs

and I may have a position for you to consider. Maybe you heard the old hospital is being converted into a wellness center?"

"I did. That's such a good use for that wonderful old building."

"Well, I'm on the planning board and we're just beginning the search for an executive director. Interested?"

"Maybe."

"At the Christmas Eve pageant Tom was going on and on about all the programs you created for that place you work for in Phoenix. That kind of innovation is exactly what we need here—not to mention someone who knows how to go after grant funding and keep the doors open."

Norah had stopped at *Tom was going on and on,* savoring the idea that Tom would show such obvious pride in the work she'd done.

"Are you available to meet with the committee day after tomorrow?"

"Sure. Just let me know what time and where."

"Let's meet at the hospital at ten. That way I can give you a tour and then the others can come at ten-thirty and we can talk. If nothing else we'd love to just pick your brain for ideas."

"That would be fine."

Norah hung up.

"Well?" Isabella huffed.

Norah had almost forgotten her daughter was there, hearing only her side of the conversation. "I have a job interview—here in Normal." Together they squealed with delight and hugged each other.

"Let's go house hunting," Izzy said as she grabbed for the phone. "I'll call Dad and see if he's free."

Caution replaced the euphoria Norah was feeling. "Iz, even if this works out for us, Dad's not moving back—you get that, right?"

Isabella gave a dramatic elongated teenaged sigh. "Mother, he *is* a real estate attorney, remember?"

Norah couldn't argue that. But was she ready for Tom to know things were moving forward so quickly? On the other hand, who better to celebrate such good news with than your best friend? "All right, call your father."

When Tom picked them up he handed Norah a folder. "Copies of your résumé," he explained. "I still had it on my laptop."

"Thanks. Izzy, you ride up front with your dad and navigate since you've got the listings," Norah directed as she climbed into the backseat. But as soon as Izzy was in the car and Tom had started down toward town, Norah sat forward in the middle, her face between them as she filled Tom in on the details of her conversation with Meredith.

Tom could smell the faint scent of the perfume she'd always worn. It suited her—it was fresh and woodsy. Totally natural. He watched her face in the rearview mirror. Her expression was animated and youthful as she recalled every word Meredith had said. And it struck him that while she had always been pretty with a sort of gamine quality to her features, maturity had made her beautiful.

Isabella called out the address for the first house and Tom obediently followed streets he knew by heart to their destination.

"Yuck," was Isabella's immediate assessment of the place. "Total drive-by. Keep going."

Tom couldn't disagree and Norah's silence said she wasn't eager to look any closer at house number one. Houses two through five were not much better. After that Norah—always determined to find the positive in any situation—began working overtime trying to find something good to say about the places.

"It has a nice yard," she commented.

"Mother, we are not going to be living in the yard," Bella reminded her as she sank lower in the seat and threw one hand over her forehead as if exhausted. "Bor-r-r-ing," she moaned.

"It's not so bad," Norah said, but even her voice rang with doubt and when Tom cocked an eyebrow at her in the rearview mirror she smiled.

"Okay, it's bad. Shall we abandon this exercise for today? It's premature."

"There's still the mayor's place," Bella murmured.

"Yeah," Tom said as he turned the car away from the street that would take them home and headed back toward town.

"We've had this discussion," Norah told Isabella firmly. "It's a fabulous house, but it's way too big and too expensive—"

"Doesn't cost anything to look," Tom said with a wink at Bella. "I'll just borrow the key from Keith." He left the motor running while he ran to the hardware store. This time Keith handed him a fact sheet on the house.

"For Norah," he explained. "Can't hurt."

Tom returned to the car and handed Norah the sheet, but Isabella grabbed it first. "Wow! There are a gazillion rooms."

"You realize this is a terrible idea," Norah told Tom.

"Hey, we saw it in the dark. Let's see what the place looks like in daylight."

"You two were there? At night?" Bella was all ears now. She sighed and returned to her scrutiny of the flyer. "That is *so* romantic."

Tom saw Norah roll her eyes and sink back onto the seat, her arms folded across her chest as she met his apologetic gaze in the rearview mirror. *Great work not getting the kid's hopes up,* her expressive eyes said.

"Look at this!" became Isabella's mantra as she bounded from room to room once they were inside the house. Within a matter of minutes she had selected her room—the third floor corner that overlooked the street. "A canopy bed would be so perfect," she announced.

"Your bed at home is a trundle," Norah reminded her.

"Oh, Mom, surely you aren't planning to move that modern stuff here."

"Oh, Izzy," Norah parroted her daughter's exasperated tone, "surely you don't expect that I can afford a mansion like this *and* all new furniture?"

Tom could not help laughing out loud at Isabella's next plan. "Grandma Eleanor has a canopy bed in her third bedroom."

"Stop laughing. You're only encouraging her," Norah warned as she brushed past Tom and started back down the stairs.

"Don't blame me. She learned this stuff from you," he replied as he followed her, leaving Bella to continue her exploration of the third floor and on to the attic.

"Meaning?"

"Meaning that from the day I met you there

was never a problem you faced that you couldn't solve. Bella has a lot of that can-do side of you in her. It's one of the things that makes her instantly attractive to other kids—that confidence and assumption all things are possible."

He saw Norah soften slightly. "That's more of you," she said. "You were the one we all turned to as kids when it looked like we were facing some impossible situation. You were the leader."

"Maybe. But we're not talking about leadership, Norah. We're talking about the ability to take lemons and turn them into lemonade. That's what you do and Bella has picked up on that from you."

"Thank you," Norah said. "That's one of the nicest things you've ever said."

And suddenly he knew that she, like he, was remembering all the hurtful things they had said to each other in the months leading up to and following their divorce. Would it always be this way? Tom wondered. Would they ever reach the point where the memories that sprang to mind weren't neatly divided between before and after their split?

Only one way that's going to happen, he thought. *Heal the split.*

He shook off the thought as well as one that had kept him awake most of the previous night—an idea not yet fully formed. An impossible idea made all the more intriguing by the sheer impossibility of it becoming reality. *What if he came back to Normal—started a little practice in town?*

"You know what I think?" he asked. "I think you need a time-out."

Norah laughed. "From what?"

"From everything. You've been worried about Isabella and then your dad and now you're thinking of making a huge life change. How about we take this evening and just put all of that on the back burner for a couple of hours?"

"You, me and Izzy?"

"You and me. Not Izzy," he replied and realized he was practically holding his breath the way he had the first time he'd officially asked her for a date when they were in high school.

"I don't know," she hedged.

"There's a new film version of that Broadway musical you like so much playing at the movies. Two or three hours of mindless entertainment with a big bucket of popcorn and a soda?"

"Tempting," she agreed. "Buttered popcorn?"

"Is there any other kind?"

"It might not be terrible," she said, mimicking their daughter.

Tom thought his heart might actually hammer right out of his chest. *Do not blow this,* he mentally ordered. "Hey, Bella," he shouted up the stairway. "Tour bus leaves in five minutes, okay?"

Norah deliberately dressed down for the movies in jeans and an old turtleneck. She was relieved when Izzy asked permission to spend the night with Darcy and Heather so they could work on the party plans.

"Going out?" her mom said when she came downstairs and laid her jacket and purse on the hall table.

"Tom and I thought we'd see a movie," she said, hoping she sounded as if this was no big deal. "Do you guys want to come?"

"Nope," her father replied. "Basketball game I want to watch. Renie, you go if you want."

"No, I'll watch the game with you."

Norah was well aware that her parents were trying to remain as casual as she was and that not one of the three of them didn't see this for what it was. Norah and Tom were going on a date. Norah heard Tom's car on the drive and was out the front door before he had a chance to come in. "See you later," she called.

"Next time, tell that young man to call for you properly," her father shouted.

On the short drive to the theater they talked

about people they'd run into that they both knew from before, amazed at how many of their old friends and classmates had moved back to Normal or never left in the first place. At the movie, Tom bought the tickets and the promised popcorn and they hurried to find seats in the already-crowded theater.

"Remember when movies didn't have commercials?" Tom said as they sat through several minutes of ads for cars, sportswear and local businesses.

"You make us sound like we're a hundred and two," Norah said, reaching for more popcorn and all too aware that her shoulder and Tom's were pressed together in the tight space. To her relief the lights were lowered the rest of the way as the feature started.

For the next two hours she was lost in a world of fantasy—the one up on the screen where people burst into song at the oddest moments. And the one in the darkened theater where she was sitting next to Tom as she had dozens of times before, laughing at the same lines, their hands touching as they reached for more popcorn at the same time. And when as usual the happy ending of the film touched Norah and brought on tears, Tom shook his head, grinned and offered her his handkerchief.

The movie was exactly what she had needed—

an escape from everything she'd been dealing with these last several days. As the credits rolled she reached over and took Tom's hand. Surprised, he looked at her.

"Thanks," she whispered.

He laced his fingers through hers and held on. "You're entirely welcome."

On the way back to the car they talked about stopping for ice cream only to discover that nothing was open in town.

"What happened to the Hob Nob?" Tom asked.

"It closed at least five years ago," Norah told him. "We had some good times there," she added and immediately wondered if Tom had taken that the wrong way when he didn't reply. "I didn't mean that…"

"I know. I was just thinking."

"About?"

"Old times and maybe some not-so-old times," he said as he drove the deserted streets and parked in front of her parents' house. He cut the engine and turned to her. "Norah, do you ever think we might have made a mistake?"

All the time lately, she thought. "Sometimes," she admitted. "But I think that's probably to be expected. I mean we were both so sure—each in our own way. And being back here—especially at Christmas—well, it's a little like the movie we saw. Not the real world." She leaned over and kissed his cheek. "We've come a long way, Tom," she said softly. "Whether it was Denver or my dad or some combination, it feels as if we've turned an important corner, don't you think?"

"Yeah, I…"

She reached for the door. "Thanks, Tom," she said. "For knowing this was exactly what I needed tonight—mindless entertainment with no pressures of job or family or anything else to think about. It was great."

She was deliberately letting the moment pass. *Opportunity missed,* she could practically hear Izzy protesting, but the truth was that she was still caught up in the romance of a world where people wore colorful gowns and sang and danced to express their joys and sorrows. That wasn't real—and neither was this.

Chapter Fifteen

The day of the party, Tom chauffeured Isabella and her friends around town to buy decorations and other party supplies.

"Aren't you coming in?" Isabella asked when Tom pulled up at the Jenkins house and left the motor running as Norah came out to help unload the car. "We need help with stuff for the party."

He kissed the top of her head. "I'm sure you and your friends have everything under control. I've got an errand to run. See you later at the party."

"Well," Izzy huffed as she and Norah stood on the sidewalk watching Tom drive away. "That errand must sure be important."

"It's probably something for his work, Izzy. Give him a break. He's been away from the office for over a week now. I can't remember the last time he did that, can you?"

"Well, it's not like anyone's forcing him to stay here. He seems perfectly happy, don't you think?"

"It's always good to come home," Norah said as she put her arm around Izzy and headed up the front walk. "Now, what are my assignments, Ms. Party Planner?"

Norah had to give her daughter credit. She and her friends had thought of everything. Although the guest list had grown to the place where the venue had been moved, Izzy had accepted every guest's offer to "bring something" and created a kind of smorgasbord of favorite dishes without either of her grandmothers having to lift a finger. The event was now scheduled to be held in the large open gallery space shared by Darcy's mom and the other artists who had studios in the same building.

"Of course, we had to invite her artist friends as well," Izzy had explained, "but the more the merrier, right?"

Before they were inside the house Izzy was already on the phone and half an hour after that Norah and Izzy had loaded her parents' car with decorations and supplies and driven to the gallery. A crew of teenagers arrived to arrange tables and hang decorations for the party. The place was alive with laughter and chatter and as she watched Izzy with her new circle of friends, Norah came to a decision. The interview had gone well and if Meredith and the rest of the planning committee offered her the job, she would take it. She and Izzy could continue living with her parents for the time being while they waited for the perfect—and affordable—house to come on the market. It was all coming together. Norah could hardly believe the changes that had come their way these last several weeks. It was like living life in fast forward, but she had to admit that it all felt right— as if some force greater than all of them was in charge.

Maybe Izzy is right, Norah thought as she watched her daughter.

"What are you going to wear?" Izzy asked that afternoon.

Norah laughed. "I don't have a lot of choices," she said as she laid out the one pair of black wool slacks, a blue silk shirt and the short charcoal tweed jacket she'd been wearing the day the call about her father had come.

Izzy moaned. "For the party?"

She had a point. Norah considered the outfit. "Maybe lose the jacket?"

Izzy wrinkled her nose. "Let's go shopping. I have the gift cards Dad put in my stocking."

"Those are for you, honey."

"And therefore I get to use them the way I want," Izzy countered.

Norah placed her palms on either side of her daughter's face. "Has anyone ever told you that you are the dearest and most generous child?"

"Not in those words." Izzy squirmed free. "I'll take that as a yes."

"Okay. We'll go shopping—maybe a scarf or necklace for the blouse?"

Izzy made a face. "Or we could start from scratch and have you wear something really hot for a change."

"Isabella Wallace! I am almost forty years old. I do not do 'hot.'"

Izzy shrugged. "You might want to rethink that."

In spite of Izzy's determined efforts to upgrade Norah's fashion, in the end she had to agree that the silver wrap dress hanging in Norah's closet was better than anything they'd seen in the shops.

"But you must have decent shoes," she'd insisted, leading Norah to the shoe department.

"It's going to snow. I can't walk through snow in these," Norah had argued admiring the way the strappy evening sandals Izzy had selected for her looked in spite of herself.

"Dad will bring the car right up to the door."

"Dad is meeting us there, remember?"

"Oh yeah," Izzy said. "He had 'something to do.' Like he couldn't put that on hold for one day?"

"Izzy," Norah warned.

But later that evening after everyone else had arrived at the party, Norah couldn't help but admit that Izzy wasn't the only one watching the door. Then just when she'd decided he'd gotten wrapped up in work as usual and felt a twinge of the irritation that had been at the root of many of their arguments in the last days of their marriage, he was there. He stood at the door shaking off the snow that clung to his hair and jacket.

Izzy's face lit up as she raced across the room to him. Norah watched Tom follow their daughter's motions as she obviously showed off all that she had put together for the party. Izzy tugged at his hand, but he spotted Norah across the packed room. He said something to Izzy, gave her a hug and moved through the throng of guests as if a path had been cleared that led straight to Norah.

"Hi." He was nervous. "Sorry I'm late."

"Hi," she replied. "They offered me the job." She hadn't meant to blurt that out, but realized she'd been wanting to tell him ever since Meredith had told her when she arrived at the party.

He grinned. "That's great, honey. Just terrific."

There was an awkward moment when she realized he wanted to hug her but instead just took her hands. He stepped back and looked at her. "Wow," he murmured.

Norah was suddenly shy under the spotlight of his gaze. *Did he recognize the dress? Remember she'd worn it when he proposed? Probably not.*

"Can we get out of here for a bit?"

Norah looked up at him. "You just got here and…"

"I know, but it's important. I've got something I want to show you."

"Outside?" She glanced at her flimsy shoes and laughed. But when she looked into his eyes she saw that whatever this was, it was something really serious—something that Tom could discuss only with her. For that she would walk barefoot through slush and snow. "Sure."

Tom found her coat and held it for her. Outside, he picked her up and carried her across the snow-covered street. She didn't protest mainly because he seemed so tense—so intent on whatever mission he was on. He helped her into the car and closed the door.

"What's happened, Tom? Where are we going?" she asked.

He forced his fingers into a more relaxed grip on the wheel. "It's a surprise—a good one, I hope."

He made turns at the next two corners and then pulled to a stop in front of the old mansion. From the glove compartment he took out a remote control and fiddled with it as he made the speech he'd obviously worked out and practiced earlier.

"Norah, five years ago I made an enormous mistake—I think we both did. But sometimes people get a second chance." He raised his eyes to hers. "I love you, Norah—have loved you even when I was so angry at you I couldn't speak. In fact, it was because I loved you that I got so angry. But it takes two—two to be together and two to come apart." He drew in a shaky breath and released it with a nervous half laugh. "I guess what I'm trying to say is that it will also take two to come back together."

"Tom, I…"

"Let me get through this, okay? Then however you decide, I'll accept. After all, like you said the other night, we've come a long way and if I'm pushing things then…" He paused as if trying to find his place in the mental notes he'd obviously worked out. "Okay, here's what I'm saying. I love you—can't say that enough. But I also love who we were when we lived here. I love the dreams we had, the plans we made, the way we were." He smiled. "Like the movie title—only real life, you know?"

Norah nodded. She felt as if she'd been holding her breath ever since he'd started to speak. She was afraid if she released it she might blow away the miracle of what she hoped and prayed he was trying to say.

He turned toward the house. "It's a big old monster of a place, but I was thinking maybe I could open a law office—"

Norah tried to quell the disappointment that pressed against her chest until she couldn't breathe. He was going to use the old house for his law practice. He was talking about moving back to Normal, but not about moving into her heart. "You're right," she said, forcing the words through a tight smile. "It would make a wonderful law office—so close to town and all."

Tom looked confused, then he started laughing and she was ready to punch him.

"I've rented office space down the street from Keith's hardware," he said. "The house—well, here." He handed her the remote control. "Press it," he coached.

Norah pressed the control and the house came alive. There was a large lighted tree in the front window. Two leafless crab apple trees in the front yard were ablaze with small red and white lights, and along the front walk and stairs gold lights glowed from under the accumulating snow. On the door there was a large wreath decorated with a wide red velvet bow.

"Oh, Tom, I don't know what to say. You did this for me?"

"For us." He pulled Norah into his arms as they looked at the grand old house. "Let's live there, Norah. Let's go back and start over and make all those grand plans we had before we got so caught up in making a fortune—me—and saving the world—you—and build the life we always wanted."

"What about your work? I mean you can't just walk away from everything you've built there in California."

"It's a global world, Norah," he said with a grin. "Cell phone, laptop. Besides, there's something exciting about the way this town is reinventing itself."

Norah couldn't help herself. This was just beyond her ability to accept at face value. There had to be a catch. "Look, if this is about Izzy—I know she's been pressuring us, but don't change your life for a thirteen-year-old."

"I'm not. I'm talking about both of us changing our lives for us. Honey, from the moment I spotted you in that airport in Denver, there's been something eating at me. When I got back to California I realized how in spite of everything I had believed, I wasn't happy. None of my success made any difference without you."

"And Izzy," Norah reminded him.

"I had Isabella," he said, cupping her face and drawing her closer to make his point. "What's been missing in my life is you—us. I love you, Norah. I have always loved you even when I thought you were being stubborn and unreasonable. The fact is that you were right. Money and success mean nothing without people you love to share them with. Please give us another chance."

Norah touched his cheek, felt the single tear that coursed the deep lines of his face and her heart broke free of the last remnants of what had been. "Okay," she said and saw that he was waiting for her to continue that with a *but*. She grinned. "No buts," she told him. "I'm saying yes."

He stared at her, disbelieving. "Really? The whole package? Marriage and all? I mean if you need some time…"

"Really," she said and then she hugged him and they were kissing and the next thing they knew a police officer was tapping on the window.

Tom broke free of kissing Norah and greeted the officer, who was clearly taken aback to discover two adults rather than the teens he'd obviously been expecting to see. "Everything okay, folks?"

"Everything's perfect," Tom assured him.

Isabella kept glancing back at the entrance to the church. Her parents had disappeared from the party shortly after her dad arrived. *Where were they?* She had the terrible feeling that maybe this was not a good sign. Her dad had been so distracted and looked so serious. *Please! We've come this far. Mom's agreed to come back here to live and I'm more than okay with that. In fact even if You decide they shouldn't get back together—and sometimes I know You decide that's not for the best—still— Please?*

The service ended in silence as the bell tolled twelve beats. Izzy tried to keep her head bowed, but she could not resist one more look back. And there they were. Her dad with his arm around her mom, their heads bowed. And then as the last toll of the bell echoed across the peaceful calm of the midnight hour, there was a moment of absolute silence and then the organist played the celebratory chorus from Handel's *Messiah*.

The church throbbed with laughter and conversation and wishes for the New Year as Isabella made her way through the throng to her parents. "Well?"

Her dad pulled a key from his pocket. "How would you like to take another look at that third-floor bedroom?"

"We're getting the house?"

Her mom looked up at her dad and Isabella was positive there were stars in both their eyes. "Yes, we are," they said at the same time. Then the miracle of miracles, her dad kissed her mom right there—right in front of God and half the town. And as if everyone had suddenly realized the significance of the moment, they broke into applause and pressed forward to offer congratulations and best wishes.

Isabella closed her eyes tight. *Thank you! Thank you sooo much for the best present ever.* And when she opened them, her parents were watching her.

"Told you God had a plan," she reminded them, then squeezed in between them to complete the circle.

* * * * *

Dear Reader,

Last December when it began snowing in Wisconsin on December 1st (and didn't much stop for three months!), I began to think about the idea of travelers getting stranded in airports. I remembered one time when I had gone to the mountains of Virginia to visit my family. A snowstorm shut down the small airport that was a couple of hours from my hometown. So, along with several fellow passengers, we hiked over to the nearby motel, only to find that they could not get their staff in to run the place. But never underestimate American ingenuity! Within an hour, we passengers were doling out linens (make your own bed!) and handling kitchen duty (short-order breakfast items only, please!). We not only made it through the night—even after the electricity and heat went off—but the following day, as we all trooped back to the airport and gradually got out on our flights, we realized just how much our lives had been enriched by the experience. Like Isabella in this story, I firmly believe things happen for a reason, and we only need to give ourselves over to the adventure of that incident to come away a stronger and better (and sometimes happier) person. I hope you enjoy this holiday story and that you and yours have a joyful and peaceful holiday season, and the very happiest of next years!

Anna Schmidt

P.S. Please stop by my Web site at www.books-byanna.com, and sign up for my e-newsletter to receive advance notice of upcoming books.

QUESTIONS FOR DISCUSSION:

1. What part did coincidence appear to play in reuniting Norah and Tom?

2. Do you believe that even random coincidences happen for a reason? Why or why not?

3. What occasions in your life can you recall where it seemed as if things were happening to send you in a different direction than you first thought?

4. What might have happened if Tom and Norah had decided to simply remain friends?

5. How might Isabella have dealt with their decision if the family had remained separated?

6. What were the factors that ultimately led Norah to decide to return to Normal—even if she and Tom did not remarry?

7. How did Norah and Tom handle parenting Isabella even though they were estranged?

8. What positive ways have you seen separated or divorced couples deal with parenting?

9. In a world where blended families are common, how can faith help?

10. How was Isabella's faith tested, and how did she deal with each challenge?

Love Inspired® SUSPENSE

RIVETING INSPIRATIONAL ROMANCE

These contemporary tales
of intrigue and romance
feature Christian characters
facing challenges to their faith...
and their lives!

**Four new Love Inspired Suspense titles are
available every month wherever books are
sold, including most bookstores, supermarkets,
drug stores and discount stores.**

Steeple
Hill®

Love Inspired. HISTORICAL

INSPIRATIONAL HISTORICAL ROMANCE

Engaging stories of romance,
adventure and faith,
these novels are set in
various historical periods
from biblical times
to World War II.

NOW AVAILABLE!

Steeple
Hill®